Fae Guardian's Poppy

Randi-Anne Dey

Fae Guardian's Poppy

Published in Canada

Randi-Anne Dey Publishing

ISBN

Paperback -978-1-0692484-6-6

eBook - 978-1-0692484-5-9

Dedication

To all those that love the rooster and the poppy-cock that goes with it. It's all about the cock baby.

Now, before you get your feathers ruffled, this is a Closed Door Romance despite the fact that Cock is mentioned 74 times.

If you haven't figured it out yet, you will soon.
Smiles :)

Thanks

Thanks to all the anthologies asking for stories!
Because of you, this story came into being.
Thanks to my parents for standing behind me and supporting my writing
(PS – Mom, you might not want to read this one!)
Thanks to my neighbor, for helping when I get distracted in my writing.
Thanks to all my editors, beta-readers, arc-readers, and proof-readers.
You guys Rock!!

Contents

Return to Everdell

Saturday, August 15

Poppy sits at the traffic light, muttering under her breath at this impromptu trip to Everdell. She had things to do, but then her grandmother had to up and die on her. She was supposed to live forever especially since she was far too young to die. Not only that, she left the farm to her and the executor had to have her out there, this weekend. Of ALL weekends, this was the worst. Dammit! Her fingers tap the steering wheel in time to the song playing on the stereo; the only thing calming her nerves right now. Not that she didn't love her grandmother. She did, it's just she didn't understand her attachment to the run down farm. A farm she had grown up on and was happy to get away from after high school.

The city is where it's at; its heartbeat a rhythm of lights, movement, and endless opportunity. Fashion design had been her calling since she could first pick up a pencil and sketch her wild ideas onto scraps of paper. Majoring in it during college wasn't just a choice; it was a declaration of her passion. And now, immersed in the city's vibrant chaos, she found herself surrounded by the perfect blend of fashion, glamour, and nonstop parties. All while getting paid to turn her vision into reality. Something she needs to get back to, because she has a show in a week. World Fashion Day. Only the biggest fashion show of the year and her ticket into the big leagues.

The light flips over to green and she pulls forward, glancing at the buildings as she drives through town. One and two stories, rather than the tall skyscrapers she is accustomed to. Stucco and wooden walls, versus sleek designs and the sparkling glass she prefers because they don't look as if they will fall down in a windstorm, unlike the ones she is driving through right now.

She smiles at the group of teenagers, dressed in ripped jeans and t-shirts. Some sporting sunglasses and ball caps. Most lounge on or around the picnic table next to the corner gas station. The local hangout because you can get anything there. Pop, chocolate, ice-cream, even a smoke or two if you beg the right person. The owner supports the kids hanging there, and did even when Poppy was a teen. Rumor has it, though he always denies it when questioned, that if the kids are there, they are not getting into trouble elsewhere and he can discreetly keep an eye on them.

She pulls up to the pumps, not wanting to run out of gas on the way to her grandmother's place. Correction, her place now. Listening to their chatter as she fills up her tank, she flips her hand over to check the time. Good, she's running on time. Twenty minutes to get there, and still have ten minutes to spare, providing she didn't get stuck behind some lookie-loo driver. Out here in the boondocks, people move at a different pace. One called slow, or a more descriptive word in her mind, is a snail's pace and one she hates. It's why she was desperate to get out after school and go to college in the city. Fast called to her and so she sought it out, much to her grandmother's dismay.

Poppy finishes filling her car and pays inside, grabbing a soda and a bag of jerky for the road. Sure, she had a cooler of food in the trunk because she was counting on spending the weekend and who knows what's in her grandmother's pantry. Jerky and soda are a quick and easy fix. Within a few minutes, she is back on the road, drifting into the past as she gets closer and closer to her old home. A home that carries many memories; most of them good, some bad, but always filled with love. One where her grandmother raised her, because Poppy was the sole survivor of a car crash that took her parents and her gramps when she was six. Ones she didn't really remember past what her grandmother had told her with each memory more like an image she got from reading a book.

She pulls up the long driveway and parks next to the other car, likely the executor's, and takes a good look at the house. The shutters hanging off its hinges, the paint peeling off the wood between vines creeping up the side. Even the roof has a covering of moss on it. A frown mars her face, trying to recall the last time she was here, and if it was this bad. Had she been in such a hurry that she didn't notice? Dammit! This would make selling it all that much harder. A sigh escapes her as she pushes the car door open, her gaze landing on the overgrown fields nearing the end of their harvest, shuddering at the thought of digging in the dirt to tame them as well. Turning, she walks up the steps, hearing them groan under her feet, suspecting the deck needs replacing too.

Her eyes drift to the swinging bench, and she moves over to it, nudging it gently. Hearing the chink of the chains as it moves. So many hours on this thing with her grandmother over the years, reading, talking, watching the sunset. Swinging gently as the rain fell around them. She blinks back her tears and rubs her eyes. Enough crying; she had been crying all week and was hitting the raging aspect of her emotions of why and how did this happen. She draws in a deep breath and pushes her emotions away. Focus on business. To deal with reading the will today, the funeral tomorrow, and listing the place for sale on Monday. Then back home, to the city, and put this place behind her.

She steps inside, memories flooding her as she walks down the hallway to the living room, filled with the antique furniture her grandmother loved. A wood framed couch with carved wooden tables on either side. An old recliner chair facing a tiny TV tucked in the corner on a side table. The white lace curtains greying in the windows and desperately needing a wash to brighten them. Turning her attention to the man entering from the kitchen, she offers him a half smile and takes a moment to look him over.

Poppy guesses he is in his mid forties, compared to her mid twenties. Chestnut hair that is trimmed in a short style; definitely out of place for the rednecks of Everdell. Hazel eyes that suit his tanned completion all with a pleasant smile. Nice black pants, not designer, but not cheap. Paired with a golf shirt in cream, the top two buttons undone. Casual but refined, she supposes. "Josh Landon?"

"Poppy McInnes?"

"That would be me, but I am certain you knew that by the pictures hanging in the hallway."

"I did, but I still have to ask. Please have a seat."

Poppy moves over to the couch and settles in. Not as comfortable as the one in her apartment, but it doesn't matter. She has no intention of staying here longer than necessary.

Josh moves over to sit in the recliner chair, picking up the stack of papers sitting on the table beside it. "As you know, you are the only living relative of your grandmother, Rose Levens. In her will, she has left everything she owns to you. This farm, its belongings and the money in her bank accounts, as well as her life insurance plan."

Poppy nods, knowing it had just been the two of them. "Yes, we lost her husband and my parents in a car crash when I was six. There was no other family. Just us. Unless you count Uncle K-K but he was more of a close friend to Grams that I called uncle."

"I am aware. What you might not know is… Your grandmother placed some stipulations in her will."

"Stipulations? I don't understand."

Josh grimaces and looks down at the papers. "I want to say, before I read this, that your grandmother was still of sound mind. She would not divulge her reasons for these conditions."

Poppy shivers, feeling a chill running through her at his words. "What conditions?"

Josh takes a deep breath. "Your grandmother has stipulated that you are to stay here for six weeks…"

Poppy jumps off the couch in shock. "WHAT!!! SIX WEEKS!! I have a World Fashion Day show to run on August twenty-first and twenty-second. I have a life in the city. I can't stay here for that long."

"I am afraid it is not negotiable. If you do not abide by the conditions and stipulations, then all her assets will be donated to the Wildwood Alliance."

"Who the hell are they?"

"They are protectors of the land around here and will probably turn Rose's farm into a national park."

"And when is this six weeks supposed to start?"

"Today."

"Fuck me." Poppy paces over to the window and glares out onto the farmland, the green leaves of the nearby oaks hinting that fall is just around the corner. The golden stalks of the hay fields waiting to be harvested taunt her. "What the hell am I supposed to do here for six weeks? There isn't even the internet!"

"Fix up the house, I suppose. Harvest the remaining crops. You can always have the internet installed."

"Right. Like the internet company is going to do that. You have seen the length of the driveway, right?"

"I did. But other farms in the area have internet now. It just might cost more."

"Yes, and with what money? Since I finished college, I had to move out of the dorms and get an apartment. Do you know how expensive they are in the city? Then there are the utilities that go with it, internet, phone, cable, hell, even garbage fees. After those, I barely have any money left over to cover fabrics that I need to buy to make dresses for the fashion show. I don't just have extra money lying around. That's why this show is so important. It's the make me or break me in the fashion industry. Everyone who is anyone, will be at the World Fashion Day show and I am going to miss it. Can't I just go do the show and come back?"

"I'm afraid not. Her rules, her Will and I cannot bend them. Your grandmother left enough in the accounts to cover expenses. She was very much aware of how neglected she let the farm get. She has granted you a starting balance of five thousand dollars. You buy what you need, and provide receipts, and you will get paid back immediately. This way, you will always have steady funds to do repairs. At the end of six weeks, the deed to the farm will transfer to you, along with the remaining balance in her accounts."

"And what is the exact balance?"

"Just under fifteen million dollars."

"WHAT? There is no way Grams was that rich. I mean, look at this furniture. We were penny pinchers."

"Despite the current condition, her farm prospered. Her soil was the best around and people came far and wide for her produce."

Poppy spins around and narrows her gaze on Josh. "Right, and that earned her millions. I don't buy it."

"You don't have to. The numbers in her account don't lie. All I can say is, I will see you in six weeks' time where I will go over everything her estate entails. Also, one more thing."

"Of course there is." She rolls her eyes while leveling a glare his way.

"You are required to call my office and check in daily."

"That's easy enough." Poppy fingers her cell phone in her pocket, knowing she could return to the city, do what she needed and come back at the six-week mark. Actually, perhaps the five-week mark. It would give her a week to tidy up. Then she wouldn't miss her fashion show.

Josh smiles thinly and points to the rotary phone sitting on the table in the hallway. "From that house line, not your cell phone. It proves you are still here."

Poppy grimaces, cursing beneath her breath at her grandmother's intelligence. "And the office hours are what, exactly?"

"Ten to five, Monday through Saturday."

"What about Sundays?"

"That's your free day. You don't need to check in."

"Of course. Not enough time for me to get back to the city and do anything of value. Even if I call you Saturday morning at ten and Monday night at five. Grams sure knew what she was doing."

"She was clever, right to the very end."

"So what happened?"

"Not sure. They found nothing on the autopsy. Just that her heart stopped, with no indication why. It stumped the coroners because everything showed she was healthy."

"Damn it. She was supposed to live forever. To come to the city when I made my break in the industry. I was going to care for her there and she could leave all this work behind."

"She loved it here. I highly doubt she would have left. If you ask me, I think that's why she changed her stipulations. So that you would see the farm the same way she did."

"Not bloody likely."

"I am just the messenger. There is some food in the pantry to get you through the weekend. Everdell runs on farm time. Most of the shops don't open till ten and close between four and five. I know city dwellers like you are used to twenty-four hour convenience, but that doesn't apply here. That's my first piece of advice. My second is, take the time to repair it. The better the condition, the more you will get if you decide to sell it."

"WHEN I sell it. Though with what she has in the bank, it really doesn't matter what price tag I put on it."

"That is true. Now, I must return to the office. If you have any more questions, just call. I left my card on your fridge and one by the phone."

"Thanks," she mutters under her breath and turns back toward the window as the front door closes, listening to the blending of the car's engine on the crunch of stone as he drives away from the house. "Why Grams? You know how much fashion means to me. Why tie me here? To this house in a dead town? I didn't even bring enough clothing to last six weeks. Some warning would have been nice, Grams! Dammit!"

Poppy spins and stomps out to her car, yanking open the trunk. She drags her suitcase out with a thud, flinching as she recalls her laptop is inside. Pulling the cooler out as well, she slams the lid and storms back into the house, locking the door behind her. Dropping the cooler at the bottom of the stairs, she heads up to her old room.

A gasp escapes her as she stops in the doorway. Her room, untouched by time. Just the way she left it when she headed off to college. A stab pierces her heart at the fact that she hadn't been back here but a handful of times since she left six years ago. Furniture painted in black, bedazzled with blue diamonds. A blue and silver bedspread with matching throw pillows, each one hand sewn by her. Dark blue and black curtains hang beside the window, bunched together, knowing in her mind, were she to spread them out, cutouts of stars would let the light in, each lined with silver threading to stop fraying.

She steps inside and drops her suitcase on the bed. Zipping it open, she pulls her laptop out and sets it on her desk alongside her phone. Pulling her clothes out, she moves to hang them in the closet, finding a complete wardrobe waiting for her; ranging from jeans and tee's to working clothes and even a few sundresses to fit her curvy shape thrown in. "What the hell?"

She pulls out a few items and holds them up against her, realizing they are all in her size. "Grams. What have you done?" Sliding the items back in the closet, her eyes drop to the boots and shoes on the floor. "Oh No, you didn't." Spinning, she moves to the dressers and pulls them open, finding new undergarments, socks, shorts and tanks. The bottom drawer contains some warmer clothes; sweaters, hoodies, and a few scarves. "Dammit Grams. Let me guess, you stocked the coat closet with jackets, too."

She backs up to the bed and slides down it, slumping to the ground. Tears flood her eyes as pain lances through her heart at everything that has happened in the past week. Her anger once more washes into waves of grief. Her rock, her support system, her everything is gone. For a reason that no one could answer.

Turning, she buries her face in her bedspread as her mind flicks through the facts. Her Grams had been healthy and fit. Not a heart issue. Not a mental issue. Even her executor had stated she was sharp as a whip up till the end. The changes in her Will, wanting her to stay six weeks. Is it because she needs to learn something? Things are not adding up in her mind.

Poppy rubs her eyes, knowing they are red and puffy, even without looking at the mirror, and yet, she does it anyway as she rises to her feet. Not the Prima-Donna fashion princess now, that's for sure. Her straight ash blond hair, cut in a V shaped bob at her shoulders, short enough to be stylish but long enough to tie up in a bun if needed. Perfect makeup, now running down her pale skin, leaving black streaks from her hazel eyes to her chin. Her clothing rumpled from sitting in the car all day, then huddling on the floor. She tugs at the lavender blouse, straightening it with a sigh, grateful none of her city friends are here to see the mess she is in. She is well below the standards the fashion industry has set right now.

She sniffles. Enough tears. Time to move forward. Her Grams obviously wants her to do that with everything she has prepared. Still, the inkling is there in the back of her mind that she is missing something. She mutters under her breath, despite knowing no one will answer her. "What happened here, Grams? I can feel it in my bones that you want me to know something. That's why you want me here."

Pulling a pair of pajamas and a book out of her suitcase, she tucks them in her arms and heads to the bathroom, dropping them on the counter. Recalling the cooler at the bottom of the stairs, she pads down and picks it up, heading to the kitchen. Emptying it into the fridge, she grabs a soda and wanders back upstairs. Her emotions can deal with a good long soak and a good book.

Fields of Farewell

August 16

The next morning, an ear-piercing scream wakes her. Bolting from the bed, she heads to the window, narrowing her eyes on a nearly dead rooster, happily screeching its morning calls far too early for a Sunday morning. She glares at it, wondering both what cooked cock would taste like and when did her Grams get the damn bird. Cursing under her breath, realizing she probably had to feed that thing, she pulls on jeans and a shirt and stomps down the stairs. Ignoring all the family portraits hanging on the wall in the hall, she heads to the back door and yanks it open, glancing around in shock at the flock of chickens all waiting for her. "Damn it Grams! When the hell did you get chickens, and what the hell am I supposed to do with them?"

Spotting a small enclosure tucked to the left of the house, she marches over to it, and steps inside. Various farming implements hang on the walls along with some stacked on work benches. To her left, she spots four large buckets nestled in the corner. Lifting the lid, she smiles to herself.

Score! Chicken feed and scratch. Realizing her happiness, she frowns. She should NOT be happy about feeding the damn chickens, let alone that potentially broiled cock.

Sighing, she scoops out some into a nearby container and carries it out to the waiting hens, scattering it at her feet. A smile creeps back on her face, watching them rush towards her, pecking at the ground. Check one for succeeding in her first task today. Putting the container back, she closes the shed door and heads back inside. Rummaging through the fridge and cupboards, she makes a list to hit the store tomorrow. If she is going to survive here for six weeks, she needs more food and alcohol. Lots of alcohol.

A couple of hours later, she leaves the house, dressed impeccably. A black fitted blazer covers a midnight blue silk shirt and the top part of black dress pants. Designer boots peek out as she walks towards the car. She reaches up to adjust the tissue stuffed in her bra, because the blazer has no pockets and her clutch is too small, especially after adding other stuff to it.

This is something she hopes to change since all her designs have pockets in her women's line of clothing. That is her defining feature, and she intends to brand it. As soon as she gets off this farm, that is. Reminding her that tomorrow morning, she needs to make a ton of calls regarding a show she is now going to miss. Hopefully, her best friend Amber can step up and take the show over while she is stuck here.

Pulling into town, she maneuvers her car towards the church, and parks it, seeing other people already milling about. She sighs as she turns the engine off and stares at the white walls with stained glass windows. Was she ready to face the entire town? Their judgments at leaving her Grams to fend for herself on the farm? Not really. She didn't love the small town feeling the same way her Grams did, and everyone else currently living here. A tap on her window draws her gaze upwards, finding her hazel eyes staring into the green ones of her childhood friend Clara.

Poppy scrambles out of the car and into Clara's arms. "Oh, my god! Clara! You're still here? I heard a rumor that you married some corporate executive and crossed the country with him."

Clara laughs, hugging her friend back. "Yes, the fast life that you crave. Alas, I am back. Apparently, my husband couldn't keep his wayward pecker in his pants. Let's count them. Twelve! After we split, the bastard even posted each of their names on social media, thanking them for spreading their legs. Fucking slut."

Poppy giggles. "Can men be sluts? I thought that was a *woman only* title."

"Alright, whore then!"

"I think the word you are looking for is gigolo."

"Nah, that's a paid exotic dancer, and he certainly didn't get paid that I am aware of. Clearly, us women need to make a name for a man-whore-slut… Either way, I received my settlement and moved back home. It's been amazingly peaceful, something I apparently needed after that nightmare of a relationship. I am sorry about Grams. How are you doing?"

"As good as expected. I bounce between anger and grief. Right now, it's a combination of both at the same time. Grams is forcing me to stay at the house for six weeks. I am going to miss the most important fashion show of my life because of it."

"Damn, why would she do that?"

"I don't know. Apparently, she changed the stipulations of her Will recently. I can't even sneak back to the city and do the show, because I have to make a daily *'check in'* call from the landline in the house."

"Wow, that's rough. She must have had her reasons. Grams knew how much the fashion industry meant to you. She supported you all the way through schooling."

"Exactly." Poppy lowers her voice so only Clara can hear it. "It's odd. I feel as if Grams is trying to tell me something that I am clearly missing. I just arrived yesterday, so I haven't had time to figure anything out, but I will. Especially since clearly I am stuck here."

"Well, if you have the time, you could come to the Harvest Moon Festival. I know its not the fashion show, but the hayrides are actually a lot of fun!"

"I don't know about the hayride aspect, but when is the festival?"

"A month from now on Saturday, September 19th."

"Yah, it's within my six week term so I can commit to that."

"Great! It's a date!"

Poppy laughs. "I might be a poor replacement for your ex, Clara. I am work driven, busy, and barely even have time for me."

"Bah!" She turns and wiggles her brow, puckering her lips out for a kiss. "I have six weeks to convert you!"

Chuckling, Poppy kisses her fingertips and plants them on Clara's lips. "Convert me? You know it doesn't exactly work like that."

"Sure, toss me aside for some man and his cock." Clara clutches at her chest in dismay. "I see how it is!"

Poppy nudges her friend. "Oh my god, you haven't changed! Thanks for making me feel better."

"My job here is done. We need to get seated before the masses arrive." Clara pats her on the shoulder and grabs her hand, pulling her towards the church.

"Right. I think your version of masses and mine differ." Poppy rolls her eyes and walks with her into the small church beside her. A rainbow of color from the stained glass windows flicker on the white-washed walls. Polished wooden pews adorn either side of the red carpeted pathway. A dark blue casket sits at the front with pale blue hydrangeas on it. Directly behind it, hanging on the wall, is a giant rosary, and in front of that stands a man talking to another, dressed in white robes. Poppy watches them for a moment, her gaze following the second man to the grand piano, tucked over in the left corner. Sighing inwardly, she moves to the front pew, seeing the white sign with her name scrawled across it and sits down in front of it.

"True." Clara settles down beside her. "But for this town, it will be. Your Grams was popular and I think everyone will be here."

"Great. That's just what I need."

Clara nudges her. "Hey, is everything alright?"

"Sorry, I just don't feel like being judged for my choice of picking the fashion industry over this town today."

"They won't. Today is sacred. It's Gram's funeral and everyone will focus on that. Now, coming into town to get groceries and such, that's a different story. If you need refuge, I work in the lumber yard in the back office as their accountant. Stop by anytime."

"Lovely."

As the pastor approaches the pulpit, the people in the church grow quiet, with only the shuffling of a movement and a few unintelligible whispers heard. Poppy keeps her gaze on the casket, not wanting to listen to his words about how her Grams is in a better place, and slowly tunes his words out as she grows lost in memories about her Grams. She startles at the gentle nudge on her side, turning her attention back to Clara.

Clara leans over and whispers. "He's done. You need to follow the casket outside and drop the first dirt on it."

"Right. Thanks." Poppy rises as the pallbearers lift the casket. She waits until they carry it past her, and steps in behind, following them out to the graveyard where they place it on the lowering device. As it settles into the hole, she moves over to the pile of dirt and picks up a handful, listening as the pastor speaks a few more words and tossing her handful in. The final nail in her heart punches into place at the dull thump when it strikes the lid, watching it scatter across the top as the tears she has been holding back spill from her eyes. She turns and flees, running back to her car, ignoring Clara's calls behind her. Guilt floods her at not being here for her Grams.

Sliding into her car, she pulls out her keys, hearing them rattle in her shaking hands. After a few attempts, she has them in the ignition, the car running and is pulling away from the church. Twenty minutes later, she is staring at the old house, not wanting to enter it just yet. Getting out, she wanders out into the fields towards the forest that borders her Gram's property, mentally cursing her poor choice of footwear. She picks up her pace as she spots the old weeping willows, ones she lived beneath as a child. Dipping under the branches, she smiles, seeing the old tire swing her parents had put up for her just before they lost their lives in the accident.

Pulling her boots and socks off, she drops her clutch and blazer on top of them, wiggling her toes in the soft moss that grows beneath the tree. She moves to the tire and caresses it lightly. Not your average car or truck tire, but one off of Gram's old tractors. She slips in and pedals backwards before lifting her feet, allowing the tire to swing as she rests her head upon it, listening to the rustle of the leaves, the gentle creak of the rope and the groan of the tree beneath its movement. She giggles slightly at the thought of the tree snapping and dropping her on her ass. It would be just her luck. An hour later and feeling better with herself, Poppy climbs out of the tire and slips her boots back on, trudging back to the house carrying her clutch and blazer.

Familiar Stranger

The next morning, she curses under her breath at the rooster crowing outside. Knowing when she gets to town, she is going straight to the library to use their internet, wanting to look up a multitude of recipes that include cock and print them off. Because before the six weeks are up, she is definitely going to enjoy some.

Getting out of bed, she pads downstairs and feeds the chickens, then whips up a quick breakfast. With a fresh cup of coffee in hand, she steps outside and settles onto the deck stairs as the morning air wraps around her. Watching the chickens peck at the feed she scattered, she finally understands why her Grams kept them. There's something oddly calming about their movements, and their soft clucking soothes her soul, like a peaceful melody playing in the background.

Realizing she has lingered long enough, she rises and grabs the list she created after wandering through the house yesterday afternoon. Heading down the hall, she picks up the phone and calls the lawyer's office, figuring she might as well do it before she drives into town. After two rings, a female voice answers. "Everdell Law offices. Celeste speaking. How may I direct your call?"

"It's Poppy McInnes. I am just doing my daily check in from my Gram's house."

"Hold on. Yep, that is the correct number. Have a nice day, Miss McInnes."

"That's it?"

"Yes. I just need to confirm the number on the call display. No need to waste time chatting."

"Even better. Thank you."

"You're welcome. Talk to you tomorrow."

"Yes, you will." Poppy sets the phone down and stares at the bowl with her Grams' truck keys. A truck that is meant for farm life, whereas Poppy's sleek car is not. Grabbing the keys from the bowl, she twirls them around her finger and heads to the garage. Slipping in, she clicks the garage remote, listening to the sound of rattling metal fill the air as the door lifts. Starting the truck, she smiles at the familiar rumble and backs out. Once the garage door is closed, she turns the truck around and heads into town.

In town, she stops at the lumber store first, wandering around to get sandpaper, a sander and paint. Once she has paid for those, she tucks the receipts away to take to the lawyers. Hitting the grocery store next, she wanders around with a cart, deciding on food and drinks. Enough for a few weeks anyhow. In the vegetable aisle, she turns over a head of lettuce, grimacing slightly at the browned leaves.

"Hey. If you want fresher produce, go to the farmer's market."

Poppy lifts her head and turns to the speaker, smiling at seeing her old teacher. "Mrs. Plum. How are you doing?"

"Great. Sorry to hear about your Grams."

"Thanks. Farmer's market, you say?"

"Yes. The old drive-in is now a daily market where farmers sell their wares. That's the place to go for anything other than canned goods, really. Produce, cheeses, jams and jellies, meats, breads. They have it all."

"Wow. Thanks, I think I will do that." Poppy looks down at her cart, deciding what to put back.

"You're welcome. A lot of them are with the times, too. They have Squares for debit and credit."

Poppy fakes a gasp, slapping a hand to her forehead. "Really? That's, like, allowed in Everdell?"

"Well, you know. Resistance to change and all… Unless it comes to collecting money."

She laughs. "Too true. Thanks Mrs. Plum."

"Your welcome Poppy. Have a good day."

Poppy moves back through the store, returning half of what's in her cart back to the shelves and leaves with her purchases of drinks, canned food and alcohol. Carrying her bags to the truck, she clambers in and drives out to the market, immediately noticing far more of the townies. Hopping out, she wanders the market, making a mental note to bring bags to carry things in. Her eyes alight on people pulling collapsible wagons behind them, thinking that's even better, being pretty certain she recalled seeing one in the garage when she got into the truck.

Watching a wagon move by her with a couple of adorable kids, she steps back, feeling herself stepping into someone. Spinning, she lifts her hand to steady them, only to find it resting on a well-muscled chest. "Oh, I'm…" she trails off as she raises her eyes to meet the man's gaze. Shaggy brown hair falling over striking emerald eyes, framed with thick black lashes and… eyeliner? Chiseled chin, and clean face, with only the hints of a five o'clock shadow. Her heart thumps as heat rises inside her. She yanks her hand off his chest despite the desire to caress it, and steps back. "Sorry, there are more people here than I expected."

"All good." He tilts his eyes, his gaze roaming over Poppy slowly, before offering his hand. "I'm Rowan. I have a booth down near the end of this row."

She stares at the hand momentarily and offers hers, feeling sparks dance through her body. "Poppy."

"I don't recognize you. Are you new in town?"

"Yes, and no. I just took over my grandmother's house."

"Ah, you are Rose Levens' pride and joy."

Poppy rolls her eyes and tucks her hands in her pocket to stop herself from reaching out again. "I don't know about that. She wasn't too happy when I left Everdell."

"No, but it was simply because she missed you. She was proud of you for following your dream in the fashion industry."

"Right… Anyhow, it was nice to meet you Rowan. I need to get some food and get back to the house."

"What are you going to do with it?"

"Eat it?" Confusion flickers across her expression at his question.

A deep rumbling laugh escapes Rowan at her expression, humor dancing in his eyes. "Well, most people do eat food. I was talking about the house. I am guessing she left it in the Will for you?"

"Right." She mumbles, a blush crossing her cheeks at her stupidity. "Yes, she did. Why are you asking?"

"Just curious."

"I see." She scans the marketplace, noticing a few around them are listening to their conversation. Not wanting to feel the shame in their gazes over her decision to sell it, she opts to keep silent on it. "Well, right now, my goal is to fix it up. Grams let it get pretty run down."

"If you need help, let me know. I do handy work on the side." He slips a hand in his pocket and pulls out a card, handing it over.

Offering a half smile, she takes the card and looks it over. "Thanks. I might just take you up on this. I am not exactly handy with tools. Fabrics is more my field of expertise."

He offers a slight bow. "I gathered by the fact you went to fashion school. I guess I should get back to my booth. It was nice to meet you, Poppy Levens."

"McInnes."

"Excuse me?"

"McInnes is my last name. Not Levens. It's my dad's name and the name on the birth certificate, despite Grams raising me."

"McInnes then." He gives another slight bow and weaves his way through people, disappearing into the crowd.

Poppy tucks the card in her purse, and browses the stalls, working her way through them all before deciding on some cheese, produce and a few oils to cook with. Balancing her supplies, she makes her way back to her truck, placing everything on the passenger seat. As she walks around to the drivers door, she hears her name and stops.

Scanning around, she inwardly grimaces at her high school rival, seeing her dressed to the nines, in high heels, a soft suede pencil skirt, and a white shirt with a matching suede blazer over it. Not exactly what's in style, but clearly expensive. She does a quick glance down at her own clothing, jeans stuffed into oversized boots and a large t-shirt, hanging to mid thighs. "Melody."

"Wow, it looks like you failed in the fashion industry, Poppy? Had to come crawling back to Everdell? I mean, just look at what you are wearing."

Poppy plasters a smile on her face. "Actually, I have my debut line coming out this weekend for the World Fashion Show."

"Then what are you doing in Everdell?"

Poppy narrows her eyes, anger simmering just beneath the surface. Forcing herself to stay composed, she grips the truck door handle and pulls it open. "I'm here because my Grams died. But I suppose you'd know that if your head wasn't so far up your ass that it blocked out the rest of the world." She gives Melody a once-over, her lips curling into a tight smile. "I see some things never change. Have a nice day, Melody." With that, she climbs into the truck and slams the door shut, not bothering to wait for a response.

She takes a few deep breaths to calm herself, instantly apologizing to the vehicle. "Sorry Truck, I know you are too old to take that treatment." Her eyes catch Melody's shocked expression as she backs away, feeling a smile creeping across her face. "Bitch! Who does she think she is, Truck? Thinking I automatically failed. Only she would be so arrogant and full of herself to not know that Grams had died. And what the hell is she wearing? Leather and suede are sooo last year! Gawd, I really need a drink…"

Twenty minutes later, she pulls up to the house. Activating the garage remote, she waits as the door rises and pulls into the two car garage. She glances back to her own car sitting outside, knowing if anything, it should be in here instead of the truck. Sighing, she shuts the truck off and clambers out, looking over at the cluttered stall next to her. Grabbing her groceries, she lugs them into the house and puts everything away. Running upstairs, she drops her purse on her bed and changes into work clothes. First thing she is going to do is make space for her car. Heading into the kitchen, she grabs a bottle of coke and moves to the liquor. Pouring a decent amount of rum into it, she caps it and tips it over, mixing it gently.

Stepping into the garage, she takes a healthy swig and sets it on the nearby freezer. "Grams, why do you keep all this stuff?" She moves over and starts sorting through the paraphernalia. Starting with the workbench, she organizes the jars filled with nails, screws and bolts. She hangs the hammers and wrenches back on the wall where they are supposed to be. Moving over to the wooden crates, she pushes the empty ones outside, knowing they can go to the barn. Finding three filled with paper, she tucks them under the workbench, suspecting it's needed for the woodstove inside.

She shakes her head at the crate full of salt licks. "Why Grams! You don't even have horses. Shit!" She runs from the garage at top speeds towards the barn and pulls the doors open. Walking down through the stalls, she breathes an audible sigh of relief and slumps on the floor against the far wall. "Damn. Thank god I wasn't starving a horse. The cock and hens are enough work to feed." She closes her eyes, breathing in the sweet hay scent of the barn, realizing that Grams must be selling the bales from her hay fields. Rolling her eyes at yet another chore added to her to-do list. "How did you do all this, Grams? I guess you didn't. That's why this place is so run down."

A quiet meow snaps her eyes open as she scans the barn, her gaze landing on a tiny orange tabby sauntering her way. "Ohh No, Grams!! You got a cat? So not starving a horse, but clearly I am starving a cat." She watches it sniff her boots, before cautiously working its way up her leg towards her hand. "If you spray me, cat, you are getting cooked with the cock. I will name it cock'n'puss, or puss'n'cock stew." Laughing at her own bad joke. "I am losing it, cat. I really am." Feeling the cat brush up against her, she reaches out to pet it, hearing its soft purr. "Well, you're pretty friendly for a barn cat. I wonder if Grams had a name for you? I suppose she did. For now, let's call you Pumpkin. I guess I will need to figure out where Grams keeps your food, or are you smart enough to show me?"

She rises to her feet, watching the cat bolt back towards the front doors. Following it, she rounds the corner into a converted stall, seeing a small bench with two dishes sitting out on it and a variety of ice cream buckets. "Well, aren't you a clever little thing?" Lifting the lid, she scoops some out and drops it in the bowl. Picking up the water dish, she heads outside to the tap. Rinsing it out, she fills it with water and carries it back inside. "Right. Another task done. I guess I should get back to what I was doing. Happy hunting Pumpkin."

Closing the doors behind her, she returns to the garage to complete her task. She stares at the salt licks, knowing without them, it might have been days before she got to the barn and discovered the cat. "Grams, you are such a pack rat." Hoisting the box up, she carries it over and drops it in the bed of her truck to donate later and removes the paint she bought, setting it on the worktable.

Walking over to the tarp, she pulls it off, gasping in shock at the old rocking chair, one she had grown up in. Running her fingers over the worn wood, she notices a slat is missing in the back. Her eyes scan the wood pile nearby and moves over to it, finding a piece that will work. Once she has attached the slat on it, not caring that it's far from perfect, she carries it back to the living room and sets it down, pushing it a few times and watching it rock back and forth.

Heading back outside, she spends another few hours dividing the stuff to keep from the items to donate, making room in the garage for her tiny car. Grabbing her keys, she pulls it in beside the truck and parks it. Staring at the pile beside the house, she groans and begins moving it out to the shed and barn. Once she's completed that, she staggers back inside and closes the garage doors. Grabbing her forgotten coke, she heads into the house and flops down in the rocking chair, her feet kicking slightly as she closes her eyes, reminiscing about days of old.

Sowing Sparks

The next morning, Poppy slams a pillow over her head, trying to drown out the rooster's morning call. Her thoughts immediately jump to the numerous ways she can plunge the cock's head into a bucket of water and drown the little pecker. Groaning in dismay, she rolls over and looks at the clock flashing 6:20 am. "Damn thing. I am still on city-time, you stupid bird."

Clambering out of bed, she stumbles down the stairs to the kitchen, and puts the coffee pot on, flopping down in the chair as she waits for it to brew. Licking her lips as her mouth waters at the rich scent of coffee, knowing that was the one thing that Grams splurged on. "A good cup of cauffé will get anyone up in the morning." Recalling how she never actually said coffee, but blended it with a French lilt. It always made her wonder if she had grown up in Everdell as she said she had, or somewhere else.

A few minutes later, cup in hand, she heads out to feed the chickens, narrowing her eyes dangerously at the rooster perched out of her reach on the shed roof, making a mental note to look into moving the shed away from her window. After feeding them, she wanders to the barn and checks in on Pumpkin, seeing her curled up on a nearby hay bale. "Hey little one. Are you hungry?" A chuckle escapes her as she earns herself a side eye from the motionless cat. "Have it your way, then." She drops some kibbles in the bowl and walks around to the front of the house, settling into the porch swing.

Her eyes drift over the fields that lay before her, ones she would need to get to if she wanted to save any of the harvest out there. "Ooh Grams. You know that I could have sold this place to someone that wanted to actually be a farmer." She sips her coffee, rolling it around in her mouth and savoring the taste, her mind drifting back to when she and her Grams sat on this very swing, talking about her desire to go to fashion school. To get out of this town that she was now forced back into. "I suppose I will never know why you did this, Grams."

Hearing the crunch of gravel, she turns her attention towards the forest that separates her from the town. Seeing a pickup truck driving towards the house, she swivels on the swinging bench and peers through the window, glancing at the clock on the wall. 7:20 in the morning. Setting her coffee on the railing, she runs around the back and into the house. Bounding up the stairs, she pulls her flannel pjs off and drags on some jeans and a shirt. Grabbing a scrunchie, she pulls her hair back in a messy bun before heading back downstairs, opening the front door just as the truck pulls to a stop.

Rowan jumps out and walks around, his eyes doing a lazy sweep over Poppy. "I know, I am early, but I was driving by and thought I could look over what needs to be done."

"I thought I was supposed to call you."

"Oh, that's right. My bad." He strides up and stands in front of her, his eyes darting to the coffee cup on the railing. "Is that Rose's favorite coffee?"

"Yes, did you want a cup?"

"I would love a cup."

Poppy heads back inside, returning a few minutes later, cup in hand, stopping to glance around when she doesn't see Rowan. Furrowing her brows, she steps off the porch and peeks around the corner, seeing him standing there, running his hands along the wood siding. "Hey."

"Sorry, I was just looking. The siding will need to be sanded and stained. There is a hole up there near the roof. Looks like a woodpecker got access to it. We will need to patch that before winter hits or you will get water damage inside when the storms blow in."

She hands over the cup and glances upward, seeing the dark shadow he's talking about. "Right, I think there is a ladder in the barn, but I don't think it's that tall."

"I have one I can bring when I get to the siding. How's the barn and chicken coop?"

"Wait, there's a coop for those things?"

"Yes. it's on the backside of the shed, tucked against the house with a windbreak. So you haven't checked for eggs then?"

"No, they were free roaming when that bloody rooster woke me up Sunday morning." Poppy rolls her eyes. "I should have known there was some place for the damn things to live."

Rowan turns to face her. "Are you having issues with the chickens?"

"Just the bloody cock. I would like to wrap a bag over its head and strangle it, or better yet, beat it till it stops crowing." She blurts out, reading the shocked expression in Rowan's eyes as his free hand moves protectively lower. Her face heats up at his actions, suddenly realizing how he took her words and drops her gaze to the ground. "No, I mean, I would… Never mind. I was talking about the rooster. He's too much of an early riser."

"And you are clearly not."

"No. City girl here. Late nights and even later mornings."

"So I am lucky I caught you awake and dressed."

"Well, I got dressed when I heard the truck on the gravel driveway."

"I see."

Her eyes lift to his, feeling a warmth flood her body again at the intensity of his gaze. "Sorry, I guess that was too much information. I just wasn't expecting anyone out here this early, so I was still in my pajamas. It's not like I was sitting on the porch naked."

"I wouldn't do it, even if you are this far out in the wilds. Lots of people wander those woods, despite it being your Gram's property."

"I guess it's been a few years. I never really thought about people trespassing."

"Well, your Grams has a shotgun hidden somewhere in the house, but she never used it. She didn't seem to mind the couples wandering through her woods. I think it helped ease her loneliness."

"Ouch, way to make the wayward granddaughter feel more guilty than she already does."

"That wasn't my intention."

"I know." Poppy sighs, her gaze drifting out to the acres of fields, tucked away behind a circle of woods, like its own private world, away from everything else. No houses on the horizon, only the sound of birds, the grasses rustling, and that damned rooster. "I just miss her. I should have called her more, or come home more often. It's just that school was grueling and when I finally got a weekend off, I either had to attend some fashion thing, or I crashed hard and slept the weekend away."

"You don't need to explain it to me. Rose was proud of you. She understood."

Poppy nods, her eyes returning to him. "I hope so. I always wanted to be a designer and she was the one that pushed me to go to fashion school."

"And she talked about it all the time. How her girl was going to take the fashion industry by storm!"

"Well, I don't know about that…"

"Only time will tell. Now, I guess we should discuss what you want to do first." He tips the coffee cup to his lips, his eyes rolling back in delight at the taste of it.

"Right." Another blush creeps across her cheeks at the thought of his lips on hers, each with the hint of coffee attached to it. "I guess the outside of the house, as you said, but I know the farm needs to be harvested. Grams has a tractor in the barn that looks about as old as her truck to cut hay. I don't want the fields seeding if people are depending on them. I know Grams kept logs somewhere, but I honestly haven't had the chance to look."

"Understandable. I will help you with the fields first. We have a month before we need to worry about rain. Does anything inside the house need fixing?"

"Besides a paint job? No. I can do that in the mornings and give it the afternoons to dry out before I have to sleep in those paint fumes. If I was energetic, I would buy a pup tent and camp out those days, but I am not."

"Or you could sleep in the barn. The upper lofts are pretty cozy, even in the winter."

Poppy arches a brow. "And how would you know this?"

"I work in one."

"Right, sorry, my mind went elsewhere."

Rowan chuckles. "Like mine did when you mentioned the wrap and smack of the cock?"

A deep blush floods her cheeks again. "Yes. Kinda like that."

"Right, well, let's focus. Then I can get out of your hair and you can return to the coffee cooling on the porch railing."

"Mine was almost empty. I will just make more later." Her eyes land on the orange tabby bounding into the fields. "You seemed pretty close to Grams. Did she ever mention the barn cat's name?"

Rowan chuckles. "Yes, it's Pinecone."

"Wait, what? How the hell did she come up with a name like that?"

He shakes his head. "Your Grams was wandering the woods and found her as a kitten tucked in a pile of pinecones. When she approached it, the little one hissed and tried to hoard them away from her. So Rose left and returned with a bucket, shoving all the pinecones and the kitten inside. She relocated her to the barn and set about taming her. In the back corner, you will probably find a decent sized pile of them."

"Wait, the cat collects them?"

"Yep. Every few months, your Grams would sneak in and take them back to the woods, only for Pinecone to drag them back in again."

"So a rooster that doesn't shut up and a cat that collects pinecones. Anything else I should know about?"

"Well, she took her wares to the market every Monday, Tuesday and Friday morning."

"Her harvests?"

"Some of them too, but I am talking about her pottery. She converted the cellar to a studio."

"No, she didn't!"

"She did."

"Right, another thing to look at later."

"There is no rush. You have time."

"I suppose I do, yes. Thanks Rowan. I appreciate the help."

"Hey, I wish I could have helped your Grams more, but she was a stubborn old… woman."

Poppy laughs at his hesitation. "I love that you changed your choice of words there. Yes, she was. You will find I am not as stubborn. I might have been raised here, but the farm life was not for me. I was inside sewing while Grams did the farm work."

Rowan chuckles. "That's good. I have the market in the mornings during the week. That's where I was heading before I popped by. It opens at eight. Afterwards, I need to tend to my place. It's not nearly as big as your Grams, though, so I only need a few hours. I can come help you mid afternoons or early evenings if that works. It's not the best time for haying, but we can make it work. Normally you cut in the morning and bale in the evening after it's dried. We will cut it when I arrive and bale it the next afternoon. It's not unheard of to do it that way and does not affect the quality of the hay."

"That sounds good. I can do any shopping I need to do in the morning. My old teacher told me the market is the place to go. After that, I will be here. I have a cell that has questionable service out here, but we can exchange numbers if you like."

"Sure." Rowan slides his phone out of his pocket and swipes it open. Moving to the contact list, he opens it and hands it over to Poppy. "I can text you, or you can text yourself if you like."

She smiles and accepts the phone, entering her number into his contacts. "I will let you do it."

"Thanks." Rowan takes it back and slides it into his pocket. "I want to take a quick look at the barn before I head off. Is that alright?"

"Yes, go ahead."

Nodding, he strides towards the back, walking around the outside before stepping inside. He quickly scans the hay bales stacked inside and spots Pinecone dragging in more treasure. Walking over to her, he pets her gently before exiting. "Barn looks good. There is an order of hay inside. I would suggest you figure out who it's for and make arrangements to get it picked up."

"Right, I don't even know where she stores those books."

"In her office?"

"She has an office?"

"Have you not explored?"

Poppy bristles under the question, tamping the anger back down. "Nope, I got here late Saturday where I met with Josh and went over the Will. Then went upstairs to my old room and unpacked my suitcase where I discovered Grams bought me a variety of clothing and had a meltdown. The bloody cock woke me up in the morning and introduced me to the fact Grams has chickens that Josh neglected to mention. I checked the shed where they were gathering and found their feed. Then, of course, there was the funeral, and I got home to another melt down. Yesterday I ventured out for food in the morning and spent the rest of the day cleaning the other side of the garage so I could park my car in it. She had salt licks, which brought on a full bout of panic, so I ran to the barn looking for a collicking horse and found the cat. Thankfully, no horses that I forgot to feed. So. NO, I haven't looked at the rest of the house. It still feels like Grams' domain and I shouldn't be snooping."

"I'm sorry. I didn't think about it that way."

"It's fine. I just got defensive, sorry. I will look for her office when I go back inside."

Rowan studies her, seeing the range of emotions race through her. "Understandable. I could have phrased it more tactfully. Here's what I know. Her office is on the ground floor near the kitchen. The keys to the pottery cellar are in there somewhere because she has some expensive equipment down there. She has containers for packing her pottery in for the market and a wagon to transport them. She sells her hay to about ten clients that I know of, and each stall is specifically designed for them. Some store it here and come pick it up when needed. There is also a back field of peaches & cream corn that should be ready in a month for the fall market where she usually sells out. The watering system has timers, so unless that glitches, you don't need to worry about that. In the barn, the equipment for harvesting is beside the tractor. People have boarded horses here, but not in a few years. It's an option for those living close to town that want horses. She has the cat and the chickens that you know of, but there are also a couple of free range goats that a neighbor pays for pasture."

"Goats?"

"You don't need to deal with them. The owner does. It's on a section of land that borders his. Apparently, those two don't get along with his other goats, so he needs to separate them. He pays your Grams monthly to do so. Just make sure you get that income because he's a bit shady and might stop paying now that Rose has passed away."

"Who is it?"

"Barney Jackson."

"Old Man Jackson's son?"

"I believe so."

"I went to school with him. He was an ass."

"Well, he still is. If you want, I can go over there with you if he doesn't pay."

"Sounds good."

Rowan flips his wrist to check the time. "I better get going. I need a few minutes to set up before the populace come shopping, and I have some things to do afterwards."

"Right, sorry for keeping you."

Rowan nods. "I will see you tomorrow then?"

"Yes, I will be here." Poppy accepts the empty coffee cup and watches as he walks back to the truck, her gaze following his wide shoulders, down to his tapered waist, before stopping on his backside, biting back a sigh of disappointment as he gets into his truck. Lifting her hand to wave back, she remains still until the truck is out of sight. "What are you thinking, Poppy? A man like that would not be interested and probably has a girlfriend." Muttering under her breath to herself, she collects her own cup and heads inside, placing his in the sink and refilling hers.

"An office, huh? Well, didn't you get with the times!" She moves to the spare room, knowing it's the closest to the kitchen, and pushes the door open, gasping in surprise. Two small lamps sit on a heavy oak desk that dominates the room. In the center, a black monitor and keyboard rest, causing Poppy to shake her head. "Wait, a computer?" Her eyes drop to the lower shelves, seeing the tower nestled into it. "What the hell, Grams? Is it too much to hope that you have internet this far out?"

Settling into the chair, she boots the computer up, glaring in dismay at the login screen asking for a password. "Dammit Grams." She types in her Grams birthday, groaning as it flashes back as incorrect, wondering how many attempts it would grant her. Pulling the drawers open, she rummages through them, knowing her Grams likely kept a notebook with her passwords. After a few minutes, she finds one tucked at the very back and smiles in delight. Flipping it open, she reads a few of them scrawled in flowing script and what accounts they belong to. "Really Grams? My birthday?"

She types it in and watches the home screen appear, along with a selfie she had taken of the two of them and printed out, framing it for her birthday one year. Tears flood her eyes as she reaches for the screen, wondering who digitized it for her. She brushes them back, fighting the sobs that are building in her chest and failing, dropping her head to the desk. "Why Grams! Why did you leave me? You were supposed to be here forever after my parents died. You promised! How am I supposed to do all this without you?" She lifts her blurry gaze back to the computer, running her fingers along her grandmother's face. "Gawd, I love you so much, Grams. I should have called you more and told you that. I hate myself for not being here for you."

Twenty minutes later, she forces herself to focus. She grabs the mouse and starts searching through files, finding a mix of things, from a folder with old family pictures, to one with word docs on what she wants to update on the farm. Realizing there is internet, she clicks on the browser and searches her history, seeing an online spreadsheet. Opening it, she reads all the entries on it. "Score Grams. Look at you, all updated and using online stuff to keep track of things."

Clicking through the pages, she reads through the list of names, phone numbers, the amounts ordered and the stalls tied to them. Her eyes dart for a phone, groaning when she realizes hers is up in her room and Grams' landline is stuck in the hallway. "Well, not that up to date, no office phone, apparently." Finding a pen, she tears out a blank page from the notepad and writes down the number of Astrid Winters, next in line to receive hay.

Opening a new tab, she looks at the other pages, realizing Grams had her college flagged as favorite, as well as a Facebook page, with the primary search being her profile. Her eyes burn as tears return, realizing just how lonely her Grams must have been that she got the internet installed and was cyber-stalking her online presence. "If I could redo things Grams, I would."

Having had enough, she pushes her chair back and stumbles to the kitchen. Pulling a Coke out, she pours a generous amount of rum into it and takes a healthy swig. Passing the phone in the hall, she picks it up and calls the lawyers, listening to it ring. When the secretary answers, Poppy mutters, "I'm still here." Then hangs up the phone and staggers to her bedroom, curling up in her bed to wallow the day away in booze and self pity.

Bender Consequences

August 19

P oppy wakes up the next morning, groaning at the pounding pain in her head. She lifts her fingers unsteadily to her temples, trying to rub away the torment, to no avail. Rolling over, she pulls a pillow over her eyes to block out the light, trying to recall the last time she went on a drinking bender, and knowing it was late teens. Her skull splitting in two at the sound of the rooster blaring outside her window. "Good for you cock. You're lucky I am feeling too ill to fillet you today." Closing her eyes, she allows herself to doze, slipping back into sleep for an hour.

Knowing she needs to get her ass in gear, she pushes out of bed, feeling the ache in her body from the booze. Stumbling down the hall to the bathroom, she rummages through the cupboards to find the painkillers. Popping the pill in her mouth, she tilts her head under the tap and takes a mouthful, swallowing it down. Staggering downstairs, she pads to the kitchen and makes coffee, looking out the window as it percolates, watching the chickens peck the dirt. "Right, sorry." Heading outside, she feeds the animals and returns to her coffee.

Pouring out a cup, she grabs some toast and settles in the office. Booting the computer up, she spends a few hours scrolling, pushing away the guilt of snooping through her Grams folders and history. Satisfied she has found everything she needs, she grabs the scrap of paper and heads to the phone. She calls Astrid first, talking briefly about her Grams and arranging a pickup on Sunday. Then she calls the lawyers, annoyed at the daily call, but knowing she was cranky yesterday by hanging up on them and owes them an explanation.

"Everdell Lawyers…"

"Hey, it's Poppy. Sorry about hanging up so abruptly yesterday. I was in a bad mood and I am still here today."

"It's quite alright. I half expected a brief call today, too."

"You did?"

"Yes, well, you called us about twenty times yesterday."

"Ooh gawd. I don't remember doing that. Was I bad?"

"Drunk, yes. Cursing us and your Grams, yes, but not so bad. Most of the time was reminiscing about things you and your Grams did."

"I am so, so, sorry. It was a really rough day."

"Hey. You lost someone special to you. You are not the worst we've had to deal with."

"Well, thanks for putting up with my drunken bender ass. It won't happen again."

"It's perfectly acceptable. We got to hear about another side of Rose."

"Again, I'm sorry. I will be normal from now on."

"Alright then. You have a good day Poppy."

"You too." Hanging up the phone, she heads back to her room. She pulls on overalls and an older shirt, then heads back downstairs to paint, knowing the faster she fixes this place up, the faster she can leave guilt-trip central. Clearing out the room, she pulls the curtains down and she sets about her task. Hours later, her shoulders spasm in pain, but she smiles proudly at the newly painted living room. She turns to wrap her brushes and clean up, just as the sound of wheels crunching on the gravel draws her attention.

Groaning in dismay, she glances at the clock, thinking she had more time before he arrived, realizing it's way later than she thought. Stepping outside, she watches the truck pull up and park, her eyes sweeping over him as he jumps out. Seeing his shocked expression, she chuckles, lifting her arms to strut her style. "It's my new fashion. I call it paint blotch overalls"

Rowan laughs. "You wear it well!"

Poppy blushes. "Why thank you. Cream is not really my color, but it looks good in the living room."

"May I come in and see?"

"Sure." She steps aside, allowing him to pass, his subtle scent of apples on the damp earth wrapping around her as she uses the door frame to support herself. Realizing he is already in the living room, she pushes herself off and peeks in, watching him examine her job. "Does it pass inspection?"

"It does! It seems all the drips ended up on you and not on the floor. Impressive."

"I've painted a lot of rooms."

Rowan turns to her in confusion. "I didn't think they allowed painting in dorms? Did you do the apartment then?"

"Yes, but… Wait, how do you know that?"

"Your Grams. She was happy you picked one on the good side of town."

"Yes, she mentioned that to me too."

"So you were saying you're a painting expert?"

"Right, yes. I helped my friends paint a lot of rooms, from high school and through college."

"Well, you've done an amazing job. What did you want me to do first?"

"I guess we can hit the fields together. I went through the office yesterday and found her list of people who normally buy her hay. Astrid was first on the list and I called her. She's stopping by on Sunday to collect it, but there are five more waiting. I would like to get that out of the way."

"I am certain they understand."

"I know. I just want it done. I hate owing people."

Rowan nods. "Did you want to change, or are you hay baling, paint and all?"

Poppy laughs, twisting her body and showing off the paint splatter on her hip. "Are you saying my designer outfit is not good enough?"

Chuckling, he shakes his head. "It is. I just know the smell of paint sometimes bothers people."

"Nah, if I am going to get dirty, it might as well only be one outfit. Let's go!"

The two of them spend the afternoon working the field, with Poppy listening as Rowan explains the harvesting process, pointing out what stalks are withering in the cornfield and which ones are thriving. He explains to her how to combat overcrowding and encourage better growth. Nearing dinner time, her stomach grumbles, reminding her that she skipped lunch and only had toast and jam for breakfast. "Sorry. I need to stop. I didn't exactly eat yesterday and only had toast this morning."

"Why didn't you eat yesterday?"

Poppy sighs, her eyes straying to the willow trees and the old tire swing she knows is hiding back there. "Some things I found on Gram's computer kinda broke me. I cracked open the Kraken rum and honestly, I don't remember anything past the second drink. Then the damn cock woke me up again this morning, strutting his stuff outside my window or I would probably still be in bed nursing a hangover."

"Is this a common thing?" Concern fills Rowan's voice as he steps closer.

"No, the last time I had more than half a glass of champagne was during my teenage years. Friends of mine were in a car crash and it brought back memories from when I was six, and in the crash that killed my parents and my gramps. I swiped a bottle from a friend's house and drank myself into oblivion. I woke up cradled in Gram's arms and still don't remember what happened. After that, I limited my drinking."

"I'm sorry."

"Not your fault. It's mine. Grams said I was always stoic at losing my parents and expected me to break a lot sooner. Apparently, she wasn't surprised when she got the *drunk and disorderly* call from the corner gas station when news spread about the accident."

He chuckles. "Ohhh, so you were a picnic table dancer then?"

Poppy laughs and nudges him. "Hey! It's a valid pastime! And to be honest, I don't know. Grams never volunteered what I did, and I wasn't brave enough to go ask Bernie."

"Bernie?"

"The attendant who was working at the time. I actually avoided him for about a month."

"Yes, I think I am with you. If I was in that situation, I would do the same. Come, let's call it a night, so you can eat and get some proper rest."

"Tomorrow I will try to be better."

He places a hand at the small of her back, and guides her towards the house. "If I can ask, what did you find that triggered you so much?"

"My guilt at being a bad granddaughter and not calling her enough. Especially when I went through her browsing history and saw Grams cyber-stalking me on my college and Facebook site, as well as flagging posts in the fashion world about me and saving them in a folder with my name." She brushes at her eyes, feeling the tears springing into them again, and averting her face away from him.

Rowan stops and places his hands on her shoulders, spinning her to face him. He places a hand beneath her chin and lifts her gaze to his. "Poppy. Your grandmother loved you. Never once did she say she was disappointed in you. It was always how well you were doing, your achievements, your straight A average, and bragging about how you were her upcoming star. She followed you to be close to you."

Bursting into tears. "I know, and I was awful because I was too busy to call her. I was too focused on my career and now she's dead and I can't tell her how much I love her!"

Rowan pulls her into his arms and holds her tight. "She knew Poppy. Trust me, she knew."

"You don't know that. I would hate me for what I did." Poppy shakes her head and sobs against his chest, feeling protected in the warmth of his embrace. Something she didn't know she needed or missed until right this moment. Several minutes later, a hiccup escapes as she swipes the back of her hands over her eyes. "Sorry, I thought I was all cried out after yesterday."

"Shh." He tightens his embrace momentarily, resting his chin on the top of her head, breathing in the mixed scent of hay, paint, and the underlying tones of white musk. "You lost someone very important to you. It's going to happen and it will continue to happen, at random times."

"I know, I just… I don't know. I want her back. I want her baby powder scent wrapping around me, telling me it's going to be okay and to smell her terrible rose potpourri that she stuck all over the house, especially in the bathrooms."

Rowan chuckles. "I would imagine that stuff is still there."

"Yes, the bowls are still there, but they are older now. It's not as strong as when she opened the fresh bags. Gawd, that stuff is awful, but she loved it."

"Can't say I have experienced it, but the house did always have the scent of roses when I entered."

"You're lucky. The older smell is far better than the fresh one."

"If I might make a suggestion, perhaps plant a rose garden in her honor. You might get away with fall planting, but spring would be better. Then use their petals for the bowls. Might smell better than the fake stuff the stores sell."

"I'll think about it. Thanks for understanding. I didn't mean to be a burden and have a meltdown on you."

"Don't worry about it. Make some food, grab a glass of water, and go soak in your grandmother's tub."

"Her tub?"

"Yes, she hired me to put a jacuzzi tub in the main suite bathroom. Remember, I said to explore?"

"Yes, well, that's Gram's room! I wasn't ready to open that door. Her office was bad enough as my first step."

"Alright." He places hands on her shoulders and steps back. "Well. Don't look then. Just pass on through to the bathroom and use that tub."

She nods, sniffling slightly. "A jacuzzi tub does sound mighty nice."

"Good, that's what I want to see. Let's get you into the house." He turns and guides her out of the field, stopping at the front door. His fingers brush a stray lock of hair out of her face. "Take care Poppy. I will see you tomorrow."

"Thanks Rowan. For everything."

"You're welcome." He turns and strides over to his truck.

Poppy chews on her lip, fighting the war within over, wanting to spend more time with him, and wanting to be alone. "Rowan! Do you want to come in for dinner?"

"Perhaps another night. I think you need time for yourself tonight. It's been an emotional few days."

She nods, knowing he is correct but feeling a twinge in her heart at his rejection. "I will see you tomorrow, then."

"You will. How about I bring a pizza that we can cook in the oven for dinner?"

"That sounds good." She watches Rowan hop in his truck and drive off, staying there until she could no longer see him. Heading inside, she kicks off her boots and locks the door, padding to the kitchen, knowing she should soak first but finding her stomach dictating her schedule. Rummaging up some food, she sits at the table and eats, her eyes drifting out over the fields from the kitchen window, squinting at the glow that seems to emanate from them. Blinking, she leans forward, seeing them return to normal. "Shoot, I am so tired that I am seeing things." Dropping her dishes in the sink, she heads upstairs to her Gram's bedroom.

Her hand rests on the doorknob, her emotions fighting her, but she pushes them aside. This is her house now, at least until she sells it. Pushing through her resistance, she opens the door and steps into the room, one that is exactly as she remembers it from when she was a child growing up. Her grandmother's baby powder scent fills the air, figuring she must have had stocks in the stuff with how much she used. Not even needing to check under the bathroom sink to know there would be at least five containers of it. The two night tables with white lace doilies, beside a double bed covered in a red and gold quilted blanket depicting a rooster. She wanders over and caresses it gently. "How did I miss that growing up?" Scanning the rest of the room, she smiles at the matching white doilies on the dressers, along with a jewelry box, a rooster figurine and a family picture, taken before her parents died.

Poppy walks over and picks the picture up, her standing in front of her parents with her Grams and Gramps on either side. Sadness floods her, knowing she should remember her parents better, but Grams was the one that raised her and so she was the one that held all the memories. Not wanting to head down memory lane, she places the picture back and heads to the ensuite.

She pushes the door open and stops in shock. Ivory counters sit on top of dark redwood cupboards, each one etched with a rooster in different poses. A cream colored soaker tub fills the room, dwarfing the toilet tucked in the corner. Beneath the towel rack, with a burgundy towel hanging on it, sits a small rollaway table with a bowl of soaps and some bottles of scented oils. "Wow Grams! It's a good thing Rowan said you just had this installed cause my teenage self would have been so jealous that you hid this from me."

She turns the taps on and sheds her clothes, dropping them on the floor and steps in as the water fills, adjusting the temp as she leans back. Once the tub is full, she shuts the water off and hits the jets, groaning in delight as the water bubbles and swirls around her. "Ohhh Gawd. I really need one of these in my apartment."

An hour later, she dries herself off and collects her clothes, heading back to her room. Dropping them in the laundry bin, she pulls on her soft flannel pajamas. Fetching a glass of water from the kitchen, she crawls into bed with a book and reads for an hour before crashing, her dreams slipping to the tall handsome helper that she spent the day with.

Reginald's Rule

August 20

She opens her eyes to the late morning light streaming in her window, a frown crossing her face at the fact that the damn cock had not risen yet. Pushing herself out of bed, she glances out into the yard, seeing the chickens already eating. "What the hell?" Bounding down the stairs and out back, her eyes scan the grain on the ground. Lifting her eyes to the shed door, she sees a white paper rustling in the wind. Padding over, she pulls it down and reads it.

Thought you could use the sleep. Reginald, the rooster, tends to be louder if breakfast is late - Rowan

"Good to know something keeps the cock from getting too cocky in the morning." She enjoys the silence, wondering what time they actually required feeding to avoid the racket in the morning, and making a mental note to ask Rowan. Going back inside, she sets her coffee brewing and makes breakfast, enjoying a peaceful morning. Her eyes lift to the blur of orange at the open door. "Oh hey Pinecone! Are you allowed in the house?" She reaches down, watching the cat approach her, twining around her legs with a soft purr. Picking her up, she plants her in her lap, feeling her paws kneading at her legs before she curls up. "I guess so."

Ten minutes later, she lifts the cat off her lap and carries her back outside and over to the barn, placing her on the table with her bowls. Dumping some food in the dish, she pats her again. "Sorry Pinecone. I gotta paint, and it's not a place for you to wander through." Returning to the house and to her bedroom, she picks up yesterday's clothes, crinkling her nose at the scent of them. Dropping them back in the hamper, she sorts through the wardrobe and pulls out another set of work clothes.

"Note to self: buy a few more clothes for working in." Heading downstairs, she glances at the clock, knowing it's too early to call the lawyers. She pushes all the furniture back in place in the living room and sets it up, glaring at the windows that had been open all night. "Good thing this is a small town. How quickly I forget to lock everything up. Tonight though."

Dragging her paint supplies into the hallway, she pulls down all the pictures and places them on the living room coffee table, starting her task for the day of painting the hallways in the house. Hours later, she stands back and looks over her work, noticing places near the ceiling out of her reach, that are not quite covered as well as she likes. She chews on her lips, debating whether to get a ladder, before deciding it's good enough, knowing most people will not even notice. Wrapping the roller up in plastic, she heads to the kitchen to wash her hands and grab a soda. Returning to the phone, she dials the lawyer's office, smiling at the secretary's voice on the other end. "Poppy here."

"Good morning. No wild stories today?"

"Nope. No more alcohol for me. For all I know, I could have been dancing naked with the cock out back?"

The secretary laughs. "I doubt it. You were very clear about your feelings towards it."

"I am sure I was," Poppy mutters. "It's going to end up in the stew pot before my six weeks are up."

"Well, if it does, please invite me over for dinner."

"I will. I better get back to my chores. Have a good day."

"You too."

Poppy hangs up the phone and tries to recall her drunken conversation, her imagination running wild as she moves out to the porch to take a break. Within a few minutes of sitting on the swing, a soft meow draws her attention. "Well, hello there, Pinecone. No, you can't go inside. The paint is still wet." Patting her lap, she stops the rocker for her to jump on. After she is curled up, Poppy sits there, watching the crows in the yard, digging at something in the dirt. Enjoying the soft breeze caressing her skin and bringing with it the scent of the fresh cut hay from yesterday.

She feels surprised to find herself looking forward to being out in the fields with Rowan again. As if drawn by her thoughts, her eyes lift to the sound of the truck in her driveway, watching it pull up and park.

He jumps out carrying a pizza box and saunters up to the railing, leaning on it as he looks at the cat in her lap. "Taking a break I see."

"Yes, I finished the hallways today."

"May I look?"

"Sure." Poppy leans back, hearing his footsteps moving through the house through the open windows. A few minutes later, she lifts her gaze to his as he steps back outside empty handed. "Looks great. If fashion wasn't your industry, painting should be."

"Thanks."

"Are you ready to hit the fields?"

"Yes, Pinecone and I have rested enough."

Rowan chuckles. "I think she would stay in a lap all day if given the chance."

"I am getting that impression. I am guessing by the way she sauntered into the house, she's allowed?"

"Yes, she is, but she prefers the barn at night."

Poppy lifts Pinecone off her lap and places her on the chair. "You seem to know a lot about Grams and how she ran this place."

"Yes. Her booth has been next to mine at the market for the past several years. We talked a lot, and I came out to help her with odd jobs. It's strange to see another person there." He grows silent a moment as he stands before her. "Everyone at the market misses her."

"Well, perhaps next week, I will bring her pottery there."

"Have you looked at it?"

"Not yet…"

Rowan nods. "One step at a time, I get that. Did you brave her room last night?"

"Yes! And that tub is to die for! I spent an hour in it before crashing. I need one in my apartment."

"Your apartment?"

"Yes, when I sell this place in six weeks, that's the first thing I am going to look into seeing if I can have it done. Doubtful though. Owners don't like changes like that."

"You're planning to sell?"

"Yes. Grams put a stipulation in her will that I need to be here for six weeks. Otherwise it would already have a *'for sale'* sign and I would be back in the city."

"I see." His eyes darken slightly as his lips purse. "Well, let's hit the hay."

Poppy giggles, a blush staining her cheeks at where her thoughts went. "I am assuming you mean the fields and not my bed. It's definitely not big enough for two. Pretty certain Grams made sure of that."

Snapping from his thoughts, he chuckles, his pupils dilating as they roam over her paint stained clothes. "I guess we will need to use my bed then, when we cover *that* hay."

"Oh." Her lips purse into an O, while color floods her cheeks.

A smile spreads across his face. "Gotcha!"

Poppy reaches out and pushes his shoulder. "You are evil!"

"That I am. Come, the light is wasting away and we have a lot of hay to bale. When is your other order leaving?" He heads out into the fields they were working in the day before.

"Sunday morning. I figured tomorrow morning I would explore the pottery cellar. Oh, and thanks for feeding the rooster. I actually got to sleep in a bit."

"You're welcome. You looked like you needed it."

Rolling her eyes, she mutters softly as she walks beside him. "Thanks for pointing that out."

"Anytime."

The two of them spend the rest of the day in the fields, getting the next order on the list ready. Once they have the hay baled, Rowan drives back to the barn with the tractor and attaches the wagon onto it, returning out to where Poppy waits. Each of them hoists the bales onto the trailer. Rowan with ease, while Poppy struggles beneath the weight of them. Chuckling, he moves over and assists her. "By the end of the week, you'll be hoisting these all on your own city-girl."

"I'm sure. I used to, but the city has clearly made me soft. Hey, did you notice the hay smells sweeter today, and it's looking better than yesterday?"

Rowan shakes his head. "Can't say that I did."

"Yes, look." She moves over to the bales from yesterday and pulls a piece out, comparing it to today's. "It's cleaner, softer, and smells sweeter." Popping them in her mouth, she chews on each one. "Today's tastes better too."

"Country magic perhaps."

"Yes, perhaps. The way the sun was shining, it looked like the fields were covered with magic last night. Then when I leaned forward, it was gone, so it was just the angle, I guess."

"The sun's light can create some amazing effects."

"I suppose." She tosses yesterday's hay stalk away and continues to chew on today's.

"Come, let's get this load back to the barn and call it a day. There is pizza in your fridge waiting to be baked."

"Right." Poppy runs around and clambers up into the passenger seat of the tractor, watching as he hops in the driver's side. Her hands grasp the seat as the tractor lurches forward, pulling the full trailer with ease. She helps him unload the trailer, leaving him to park the tractor while she runs inside. Preheating the oven, she finds her Grams' stoneware and places the pizza on it. Stuffing it in the oven and setting the timer, she pulls out a couple of sodas and sits at the table just as Rowan steps in the back door. She smiles up at him, sliding a drink his way. "Coke?"

"Sure." He sits in the chair and glances around the kitchen. "What color do you plan on painting the kitchen?"

"I don't think it needs to be done. It still looks pretty good, actually. Same with the office."

Standing up, he moves to a few of the cupboards. "Some of these hinges need to be adjusted to make the doors swing better. I have tools in my truck and can do that if you like."

"Right now? Are you not exhausted?"

Chuckling, he turns to face her. "I am not a city boy. This is my life. A few hours of baling hay is nothing."

"Speak for yourself."

"I am. I will be right back." Rowan heads out to his truck and returns a few minutes later with a large, dented metal box. Setting it on the floor, he opens it and rummages through it. Finding the tools he needs, he sets about fixing the cabinets.

Poppy watches his backside, the way his muscles flex in his arms and across his shoulders, wondering what it would feel like to run her hands over them. Her eyes catch the slight hint of ink at the base of his neck, curious as to what image he has etched permanently into his skin. A smile crosses her face as she recalls the fad when they were old enough. All her friends went out and got wolf tattoos. She hadn't been brave enough to face the needles and played hookie that day. If she had, she would be sporting a full moon on her back with a sword driven through it, stars surrounding the outside, and somewhere in there, the color blue. Not that she was ever going to have the courage to do that.

The timer startles her out of her thoughts, her eyes darting to the stove. Jumping up, she slides the oven mitts on and pulls the pizza out, placing it on the top and taking in a deep sniff. "Perfection!" Opening the newly fixed cupboard, she pulls out two plates and sets them on the counter. Moving to the drawers beside the stove, she rummages through them until she finds the pizza cutter and slices it up. "Help yourself."

Rowan drops his tools in the box and moves to the sink, washing his hands. Grabbing a plate, he slides a few pieces on and hands the plate over to Poppy. Collecting the second plate, he fills it and carries it back to the table. "It does smell good."

Poppy accepts the plate and sits with him, placing it on the table. "Pizza is not that hard to cook."

"I don't know. I have seen some pretty black crusts in my day."

"It's the stoneware. It never burns things and is the best thing to cook on."

"Might have to look into getting one."

Poppy moans in delight at the taste of ham, pineapple and cheese, blending with the tomato sauce and oregano. "It's been so long since I had homemade pizza. The cities are all quick and taste like cardboard. I tend to gravitate to other foods, like poké bowls, because of it."

"What is a poké bowl?"

Poppy laughs softly. "Right, small town. Poké is raw fish, usually salmon or tuna, in a flavored sauce, over rice. Some places add avocado, or shiitake shrooms." She points to the pineapple. "I've even had one with mango and pineapple. It was actually pretty good."

"Raw fish? Sounds disgusting."

"Yes, similar to sushi, I suppose."

"I can guarantee there is none of that in Everdell either."

"Well, someone needs to open a restaurant."

"There would be no point, especially since you would be the only one eating it, and you're leaving in six weeks." A slight edge creeping into his voice at his words.

"Hey, I can still crave it in the meantime." Poppy scowls slightly his way.

Rowan rises and carries his plate to the sink. "True. I should go."

Poppy rises, feeling the shift in the air. "Is everything alright?"

"Yes, it's fine. I just remembered I have some things to do to get ready for the market tomorrow."

"Alright. Thanks for the help today."

"You're welcome. I will see you tomorrow."

"Tomorrow I will actually be busy. The launch of my fashion wear is tomorrow afternoon at the World Fashion Day show and all day Saturday."

"Are you leaving town then to be there?"

Poppy rolls her eyes, an edge of bitterness slipping into her voice. "No. Grams put a stipulation that I have to call the lawyers from the house phone every day except Sundays. There is not enough time. Even if I called at ten tomorrow morning and drove the three hours back to my apartment, collected my things, then another hour to the show, I still need to call sometime on Saturday. Since the show is both Friday and Saturday and goes till nine at night both days, there is no way I am making it back to call them by five on Saturday in time for their deadline. Let alone going to the after parties that are mandatory. Even Sunday, there are lunch gatherings where you meet other designers and discuss options of working together. It's a huge event and I am missing it."

"I'm sorry."

"It's not your fault. It's Gram's stipulations and the damned lawyers. He wouldn't even grant me the weekend. He could have said," She air quotes her hands. "*Okay, you can go do your fashion show on Friday and Saturday, then return late Sunday evening but I expect a call first thing Monday morning.* Really, what are two or three days in the grand scheme of things?"

"There is always next year."

"I suppose. The fashion world is cutthroat and by then, someone could have stolen my ideas. The mentors try to snap up the upcoming students in the first year out of school. It's heartbreaking, but it's my issue. I will see you on Monday?"

"Monday it is. Have a good weekend Poppy."

"Thanks." Poppy follows him to the door, leaning against the frame as he drives off. She sighs inwardly, mentally going over where things went wrong. It couldn't have been the sushi talk, so it must have had something to do with her leaving. Sighing outwardly, she closes and locks the door. Glancing at the living room, she closes all the windows downstairs, sliding their latches into place. Once everything is secure, she grabs a glass of water and heads upstairs to the soaker, thinking it's the best thing since sliced bread after a hard day's work.

After her bath, she picks up her phone, surprised to see hundreds of messages asking where she is, followed by panic that she's not answering or replying. Her brows furrow, trying to recall when she last picked it up, knowing in the city she lived for her phone. Shaking her head, she plops herself down on her chair in front of the desk and rifles through them, answering the most important and leaving the rest till tomorrow. Opening her lap-top, she boots it up, and runs downstairs to Grams' office, needing the Wi-Fi password. The internet here on the farm is certainly an unexpected happy surprise.

The only reason she packed her laptop is because it contains all the designs she created for the show. Which is another thing she has not looked at in five days, and if she is being truthful, clearly not missed it. Sighing inwardly, she putters for an hour, sending messages to Amber about taking over the show for her. Explaining that she needed to stay on the farm for six weeks before she could return to the city. She then sends an email to her neighbour, asking if she could go in once a week and water her plants, knowing she had a key just for that very reason. Afterwards, she shuts it down and curls up in bed, feeling the exhaustion in her body, as sleep pulls her away.

Rooster Revelations

She wakes in the morning, groaning in dismay at the yodel coming in her window. "Yes, you practice that screech, you damn cock. When I get my hands on you, you're gonna need it." Pushing the covers aside, she groans at the ache in her muscles. Two days of painting and baling hay is getting the better of her. She runs her hands through her hair, knowing it's a disaster. Gone is the chic slick look, the hours spent with mousse and gels to make it lie perfectly. Now it was more bed head and messy bun.

"Great Poppy. How quickly we slip back into the farm girl. Only five more weeks, and we can go back to normal." She looks at her manicured nails, chipped, broken, wondering if Everdell has advanced enough to have a nail salon. Something to look into on Monday. Hearing the rooster call again, she clambers from the bed. "I'm coming, you stupid cock!"

She pads downstairs and out the back door, heading straight for the feed to shut the bird up. Once fed, she wanders around the back to look at the chicken coop, seeing a few hens roosting inside. "I guess I will need to Google to find out how to tell what eggs are edible, especially since there is a cock here. Lord knows just how busy he's been with all you resident chicks."

Her eyes land on the cellar doors, knowing she should contact people about the show, but it's not like they would even be awake yet. Running back inside, she searches for the keys in the office. Finding a set hanging on a hook, she carries them back, twirling them around her fingers. Finding the right one, she opens the cellar doors and walks carefully down the stairs.

At the bottom, she searches for a switch and flips it on. Fluorescent lights flood the room, illuminating the pottery wheel in the center and the shiny kiln with clear venting to the outside somewhere. Tucked in the corner are stacks of clay, still in their original bags. Nearby, a few pottery items sit on what appears to be a drying table. She walks over and picks one up, looking at the intricate details her Grams had carved into them, let alone actually making the pot itself.

Setting it down carefully, she walks over to the rubber containers. Kneeling down, she opens the first one and unwraps one of her pieces; a coffee mug with metallic red, green and blue swirls set into the feathers of a rooster, against the tan pottery color. Placing it to the side, she rummages through and looks at a variety of other pieces, each one containing a rooster in some shape or form; some just the heads, others the full bodies from perching to pecking. She carefully wraps them back up and tucks them back in the box, all except the coffee mug. "Wow Grams. This is amazing. I didn't know you liked cocks so much."

Carrying the mug outside, she locks the cellar up and heads to the kitchen, placing it on the table while she brews coffee. Once it's ready, she carries it, along with some breakfast, back to her bedroom, and boots up her laptop. Checking the time, she realizes it's still too early to call anyone in the city, so she turns her focus to refining her speech. She tweaks the wording and adjusts it to reflect the fact that she won't be the one delivering it. Hopefully, her college bestie will. Satisfied with the revisions, she flips back to her designs, jotting down notes about each one. Once everything is polished to her liking, she attaches the files to an email, gives it one last glance, and hits send.

Picking up her phone, she moves it around her and scowls at the lack of service, muttering softly beneath her breath about being stuck on a farm in the middle of no-man's-land. Typing into her keyboard, she searches for Amber and video calls her instead, knowing that with the show today and her own line to debut, she should be up by now. At least she had the internet to do that.

Listening to the chime ring, she taps her chipped nail on the desk, feeling pain in her heart that she is not there in the city with her. The screen flashes open, and Amber answers, clearly having just rolled out of bed, with her normally coiffed auburn hair tied up in a ponytail, with stray strands sticking out everywhere, and her freckled face makeup free. Poppy smiles as her face brightens with excitement at seeing her on the other side of the screen. "Amber!"

"Poppy! Why the hell are you stuck in the boondocks?"

"Grams. Apparently, she put in her Will that I need to stay here for six weeks. I was less than thrilled to find that out."

"Couldn't you just come for the weekend?"

"Alas, no, I have to call from the landline every day between the hours of ten to five to inherit this place, or the whole inheritance goes to some tree hugging hippies."

"Damn really?"

"Yes, really. So I am calling to ask you for a huge favor. I know you have your own line coming out, but can you cover mine, or find someone you trust to cover it?"

"Yes, I got your email from yesterday, late last night. Happy to help. I can get my brother to manage my line and I can do yours. Especially since mine is men's clothing and yours are *pockets*!"

"Well, it's more than pockets. It's fashionable too."

"Yes, but we need more ladies' clothes with pockets, so it's still pockets! I can't wait to debut it."

"Just remember, they are my pockets."

"Ya, ya, I got you Pop!"

"Thanks Amber, I really owe you. I just sent another email with all the descriptions and what I would like said."

"On it. I have it open right now and am reading it. This is gold. I should get you to write about my line."

"You let me know, and I will. It's the least I can do."

"So six weeks, huh? That's rough."

"Yes, a bit. There is a lot to do here. Grams let the place get really run down, and it needs to be fixed up before I can list it. Also, there are some outstanding orders that need to be fulfilled by harvesting the fields. So that's what I am doing." Poppy leans back in her chair, shifting her gaze towards the window. "Besides, there is a pretty hot local that's been helping me out."

"Ohhh Poppy! Do tell!"

"Taller than me, but not too much. Enough to rest my head in the crook of his neck. Dark brown hair with the most amazing green eyes you have ever seen. Great build and arms that hold you close and make you feel safe. I've seen hints of a tattoo on his back, right at the neckline, but he keeps his shirt on... Unfortunately. He smells like apples after they have fallen to the ground in the fall, and the damp earth. It's hard to explain."

"Apples? Really?"

"Yes, it's crazy. If you told me a man smelled like apples and dirt, I would have rolled my eyes and scrunched my nose, but it's so unique and it suits him. It's comforting, like when Grams made her apple pie."

"Wow Poppy, it sounds like you have a crush on him. Has he kissed you yet?"

"Not yet."

"Yet? So you want him to kiss you?"

"I wouldn't be opposed to it."

"So.. it's been a week, Poppy. Is he not straight?"

"I'm pretty sure he is. I've seen the way his eyes roam over me, but I haven't exactly been my designer self." She sighs and fiddles with a pen on the desk. "When he gets here, I am covered in paint, no makeup, my hair in a messy bun. Then we head to the fields to bale hay until dinner."

"You have a natural beauty Pop, he would see that. Perhaps invite him in for dinner."

"I did that. We had pizza last night."

"And still no kiss?"

"No, I don't know. It was going well, and then he distanced himself and left with an excuse of having to do something."

"Hmm. When is he there next?"

"Not till Monday."

"Well, perhaps you need to step up your game."

"I will think about it. Anyway, I should let you go get ready. Thank you again for taking care of my show."

"No problem! The fashionista Poppy McInnes owes me one. I love it!"

"I do."

"Hey before you go! Perhaps labor day weekend, I can drive up and we can have a girls' weekend? Maybe meet this man of yours."

"He's not mine, and it sounds like a plan. Clara, my high school friend, is back in town, too."

"Ooh, I feel like I know her already. Do it! Invite her. We can have a chick-flick movie and wine weekend."

"Alright, I will set it up."

"Great. I will call you Sunday night with the results."

"Thanks." Poppy disconnects the call and rises from her chair, moving over to her window. Her eyes scan the fields, seeing the hay blowing in the breeze. Knowing she has a few hours before the show starts, she pads over to the closet. Pulling off her pajamas, she tosses them on the bed, yanking on jeans and a button down shirt. She runs a brush through her hair, taming its wild strands along with dabbing some pink gloss on her lips and mascara on her lashes. Feeling a little more normal, she grabs a pair of hiking boots and carries them downstairs, pulling them on.

Heading outside, she wanders the land and looks over the crops, weirdly certain that they are thriving more today than they were yesterday. Ending up near the back fields, she spots the goats grazing next to the creek that borders Gram's property. Approaching them, she watches them wander the field, her eyes glancing towards the farmhouse in the distance. One she avoided growing up because of who lived there and one she might need to visit if Barney reneges on her payments. She certainly hopes not.

Turning around, she moves along the water's edge, smiling at the line of willows ahead of her, and the tire swing that lies hidden in them. Her fingers caress the branches as she slips through them, having spent a lot of her young life beneath them. Willows were her favorite tree, and Grams has about fifteen of them along the river's edge. Add that to the clumps of pussy-willows growing at the edge of the water beneath them and it's a recipe for happiness. Finding her swing, she slips into it and kicks back, allowing the flow of movement to soothe her soul.

Closing her eyes, she keeps pedaling and swinging until the sound of hoofbeats pulls her from her trance. Slipping from the tire, she moves towards the river, scanning out into the woods, spotting Rowan on the back of a beautiful black Friesian. Dressed in black jeans that appear to be a faded grey in comparison to the richness of the horse's coat. His white shirt, complete with tassels, clashes against the black mane resting against it. Bright green cowboy boots stand out, looking out of place, but knowing they match his eyes perfectly.

Heat floods her body at the sight of him, feeling an instant well of desire rise within her along with the urge to climb up onto the horse with him and forget everything; her stresses, her worries, to ride into the sunset, and leave reality behind. To feel his lips on hers, his body against hers, and confirm what she already suspects; that his cock is far less irritating than the one that crows at dawn every morning. In fact, she'd wager everything she owns, or will own, that his would be infinitely better.

Her cheeks flame at her thoughts and she lowers her gaze to the ground, knowing she doesn't have a right to fantasize about him that way. Muttering under her breath. "Get a hold of yourself, Poppy. A man like that is going to be taken." Feeling a shiver run through her, she lifts her gaze, locking her hazel ones onto his green ones, feeling her core fire up at the thoughts flooding her mind. She hesitantly lifts a hand and waves, knowing she told him she was busy all weekend. "Hey."

Rowan turns his horse and walks toward her, guiding him carefully through the creek, and ducking under the willow strands. "I thought you had your debut today?"

"It is. But city time starts later, so I thought I would wander to wear out my nerves. Shouldn't you be selling your produce at the market today?"

"I took the day off." He nods, his gaze moving down over her body, from the styled hair to the hiking boots at her feet. "Did you have time for a ride?"

"I…"

"No pressure Poppy."

Mentally debating the pros and cons, she glances back toward the house. "I would love a short ride, providing we are back by two when the show starts. I have already been wandering for who knows how long and I didn't bring a phone or watch."

Rowan lifts his wrist and tilts it, reading the time. "It's almost noon. I can get you home by one, so you have time to make lunch before your show."

"Sounds good, but I suppose if I am going to be out of sight of the house, I should lock it up."

Rowan slides off the horse and moves to stand before her. "We can stop by there first."

"Sure."

"Alright, let's get you up on Ebonwind." He guides her over beside him, then lifts her by the waist and places her in the saddle. Pulling up behind her, he settles in and wraps his arm around her, taking the reins in his other hand. Lifting them lightly, he urges the horse forward, cantering at a gentle speed back to the house. Once there, he assists Poppy down and waits for her to lock the house up. Lifting her back up in the saddle, he asks. "Where do you want to go?"

"Wherever you want to take me. It's been years since I explored the land. Even then, it was mostly the corner gas station."

He chuckles, pulling himself back up into the saddle behind her. "Except for the month you avoided it."

A blush stains her cheeks. "True, but I hid in the house for the month just to avoid people."

"Have you been to the lake?"

"Yes, but I don't remember it. Grams said my parents took me there when I was a kid. She offered, but I always declined because I knew she had a lot to do on the farm, and wanting to spend the day at the lake wasn't fair to her."

"It's not fair to you either. To miss the fun that could be had at a lake as a kid."

"I don't think I was the most chipper child. Especially since I lost my parents and my gramps in a car crash that I barely survived... Wait, isn't it an hour away?"

"By road yes, because you have to go around the property lines, but there are trails to it. It's about a twenty-minute ride through the woods."

"Is it alright to ride on someone's property? I mean, I know Grams allowed it, but Mr. Jackson hated us even placing a toe on his land."

"It's my land we are crossing, and I allow it." He winks at her.

"Well, isn't that generous of you?" She teases him gently. "I didn't know you bordered Grams."

"Just the backside and only a small section."

Poppy chews on her lip, glancing out towards the landscape. "Sure, let's do it. Should I grab a swimsuit?"

"Next time. This is just going to be a ride by."

"Deal."

Rowan smiles and pulls her close against him, guiding Ebonwind around and out towards the woods, galloping him smoothly across the hayfields. Entering the woods, he walks him along the trails, pushing away the branches before they slap them in the face. Enjoying the feel of Poppy pressed against him, the sweet scent of her perfume wrapping around him.

Poppy watches the woods pass, feeling a comfortable lull in her body as she leans against Rowan, a pleasant contentment filling her as if this is exactly where she is meant to be. She closes her eyes, listening to the plodding hooves, the sounds of birds chirping in the woods, the rustle of the wilderness in the breeze floating over her. Her mind fills with questions, but her mouth fails to ask them.

Twenty minutes later, peals of laughter break the silence as they clear the forest onto the grassy shores by the lake. Poppy straightens in the saddle, taking in the chaos before her, feeling her heart sink at her dreams of having private time at the lake shattered. Having forgotten that it's late August and that kids are out of school; watching them happily race around, in and out of the water, a lot of them with water wings, a few even with life jackets. The older children are just as rambunctious in their own way, as they swim with their friends out to the raft and back, racing each other. Teenagers linger on the shore in groups, some wading up to their knees as they laugh and talk amongst themselves. Some adults lie on towels, sunbathing with a book in hand while parents sit on blankets, surrounded with baskets and toys, as they observe their children play. "Wow, it's busy here."

"It usually is in the summer. The bonus with Ebonwind is we can ride to the other side, where they can't drive and very few feel like walking. Because of that, most stay on this side of the lake with the dock and raft they can frolic around."

Poppy shivers at his lips next to her ear, closing her eyes at his closeness, her hands tightening on his arms. "Sounds good."

"ROWAN!" a voice calls out.

Poppy turns her gaze behind them, her heart plummeting at seeing Melody jogging their way. "Lovely." She mutters softly beneath her breath.

"Ooh Poppy, I didn't see you there."

"I'm sure you didn't."

"What are you doing with my man?"

Poppy stiffens at her tone and adjusts her body to meet Rowan's gaze. "You're with her?"

Rowan narrows his eyes, and gives a shake of his head, his voice quiet and only meant for her. "No, I'm with you." Turning back to Melody, his voice cools. "What do you want, Melody?"

"You know what I want." Melody places her hands on her hips, toying with the laces on her bikini. "Why is she on your horse?"

"Because I invited her for a ride."

"I've been asking for months." Her lips pucker as she pouts, batting her lashes at him.

"And you can keep asking. The answer is always going to be no."

Glaring at Poppy, she points a finger at her. "What does she have that I don't?"

"Do you really want that answer?"

"Yes!" Melody stamps her foot as she glowers at Poppy, sitting where she wants to be with her back pressed against Rowan, his arms wrapped around her and clearly more content than she deserves to be.

"Because Ebonwind is finicky and Poppy can control what's between her legs." Rowan turns Ebonwind around and gallops away down the shoreline, smiling at Poppy's laughter in front of him. "It's nice to hear you laugh."

"I haven't really had much to laugh at, all things considered, but that was priceless. The look on her face! Damn, I wish I had my phone and caught that on camera." Laughter escapes her again as the image burns in her mind. "I hope I didn't make trouble for you."

"You didn't. It was only a matter of time before she set her sights on me. Perhaps now she will shift them to someone else."

"Doubtful. Melody has always been a joy leech and misery magnet, even in school. No matter what you did or succeeded at, she was always there to tear you down. I am surprised she's still here, actually. She always bragged about landing a rich billionaire and marrying into money."

"Rumor has it she left and came back several months later with her tail tucked between her legs. Since then, she's been working her way through the eligible bachelors of Everdell."

"I see." Poppy fights the jealousy in her heart at the thought of Rowan and Melody getting together.

Rowan slows Ebonwind down to a walk. "By the subtle stiffening of your body, I don't think you do. I was never eligible for her and never will be."

Twisting around to try to face him, she lifts her gaze to his. "What do you mean?"

Rowan smiles, pulling Ebonwind to a stop and looping the reins over the saddle-horn. Sliding from the saddle, he lands on the ground. Reaching up, he places his hands on her waist and guides her slowly from the saddle. "It means Poppy that there is no place in my heart for her."

She feels the closeness of him as he pulls her off, looking up into his gaze. "Does someone else have it?"

"Not yet, but there is this messy haired, paint covered blonde that's creeping in and she bales hay like a pro. I haven't seen her today, but perhaps you can guide me in her direction."

Poppy laughs and nudges him gently. "It's World Fashion Day! She's in hiding. Could you imagine if that look got out?"

"I don't know. I think it's kind of cute." He reaches up to handle the hair framing her face, feeling its softness as he tucks it behind her ear. His fingers brush over the skin on her ear and down along her throat, lingering at the silver chain there. He wraps his hand around the back of her neck, burying his fingers in her hair as he tugs her close, his lips finding hers.

Poppy feels the flames in her body at his touch, the gravitational pull towards him growing with each second that passes. Lifting her eyes to his, she feels him tug her closer, seconds before his kiss floods her with desire. She sinks against him, her hands twisting in his shirt as she responds to his lips on hers, creating stronger feelings within than she could have imagined.

Rowan pulls back and stares into her eyes, cupping her face in his, his eyes twinkling as a smile flashes across his face. "I suspect I shouldn't have done that, especially since I am interested in this paint covered farm girl."

Poppy blushes. "Well, I won't tell her if you don't."

"Good." He pulls her back and kisses her again, this time taking full advantage of Poppy's willingness. He groans and pulls away from her lips, wrapping his arms around her and holding her tight against him. "I should get you home."

Poppy struggles with the disappointment at his withdrawal, but nods. "I suppose. It's probably getting close to that time."

"It is, and I made you a promise." He lifts her back up on the horse, his hands lingering a moment before pulling himself up behind her. One arm snakes around her waist and holds her tight while the other picks up the reins. He urges Ebonwind forward with a squeeze of his muscular thighs, guiding him towards the farm.

Each of them ride in silence, lost in their thoughts about what just happened on the shores of the lake. At the farmhouse, Rowan dismounts and helps Poppy down, walking her to the front door. He touches her cheek lightly. "Good luck on your debut. I will see you on Monday."

"Thanks for the ride, Rowan."

"Anytime." He leans in and kisses her lips lightly, then places a second one on the tip of her nose. "I expect to see my farm girl on Monday with exciting stories to tell me."

"Let's hope so."

"If your style here is any indication, you got this in the bag."

Bursting out with laughter, she pushes him away. "Go! You are too evil for the likes of me. I've got standards!"

He chuckles and mounts up, turning in the saddle to face her, winking. "I know. That's why I like the farm girl." He urges Ebonwind once more into a gallop and races off down the driveway.

"I WILL GET YOU BACK ROWAN!!!" she yells out after him, watching until he's out of sight.

Fashionable Stranded

August 21 - 23

Turning, she unlocks the door and bounds into the house, dancing around as she recalls the kiss and the happiness that fills her heart. In the kitchen, she peers out the window, watching the chickens wander around, her eyes landing on the rooster perched on the top of the shed. "I might even tolerate you today, cock, so you better take advantage of my good mood." Once her sandwich is complete, she grabs a soda and carries it and her plate back to the phone. Picking it up, she calls the lawyers. "Poppy reporting for duty."

"Duty acknowledged. Have a good day."

Smiling, she hangs up and snatches her food, heading back to her room, where she settles in for the afternoon. Watching the videos and commentary of the fashion show, a part of her desires to be there, while the other part wants to be with Rowan at the lake. Pulling out her sketch pad, she haphazardly doodles, her eyes watching the runway models strut their stuff. She mentally critiques the fashion, deciding what she likes in the outfits and what she doesn't, how the fabric flows in the walk and what looks stilted, already coming up with ideas for her next show.

A large smile crosses her lips as her first design hits the runway, loving the teardrop neckline and the dark blue fitted bodice, adorned with embroidery to make it appear as if the model is wearing a corset with an ornate busk of keys and locks. A flowing skirt floats down to the models knees, lightening in color as it descends to the hemline. Her eyes shift to the crowds she can see, watching their pens move, and the cameras flash, grateful that she isn't seeing any pursed lips or looks of dismay.

Hours pass as each design comes out, cheering inwardly for her creations and Ambers, along with another colleague that she was not as close with. Hoping that each of them make it into the industry. As the runway shuts down for the dinner hour, Poppy stretches and runs downstairs, too excited to feel hunger but knowing she should eat. Quickly putting together some dinner, she bounds back upstairs, munching on her food, and she opens another tab to scroll through comments, liking every one that commented on her designs.

She flips back to the runway videos when the announcer comes through her speakers. Hours later, she sits in euphoric contentment at the triumph the show was. Knowing tomorrow is a new day and hoping that her success continues. Collecting her plate, she heads downstairs and sets the dishes in the sink. Hearing the subtle meow from Pinecone, she opens the door and lets her in. "What's up, pussycat?" Picking her up, she cuddles her for a moment and places her back down, washing her dishes.

Once they are drying in the rack, she heads outside to sit on the deck stairs, feeling Pinecone rubbing against her. "Oh, did I not give the pussy enough attention today? Come on then. Hop on." She shifts her legs, feeling the weight of Pinecone as she settles in her lap. Hearing her purrs as she watches the sun set over the land, bathing everything in a golden haze with the rolling fields of hay, wheat and corn appearing to catch fire in the waning light. The warm air cools around her as dusk settles in, carrying the distant sound of crickets and frogs tuning up for the night.

Thirty minutes later, she places Pinecone down and steps inside, watching her bound over to the barn. Smiling, she closes the door and sets about locking up for the night. Once secure, she heads upstairs to bed, knowing she should soak or shower, but wanting Rowan's lingering scent on her for just a bit longer. Falling into a deep sleep with dreams of a dark-haired knight, riding up to her castle, dressed in Amber's modern designs, saving her from the monsters lurking in the shadow.

Saturday morning, Poppy opens her eyes and stares at the ceiling, excitement filling her as thoughts of the show flood her mind, tuning out the rooster yodeling outside. Pushing herself out of bed, she races down to the kitchen and sets the coffee to brew. Opening the back door, she steps out into the morning sun, pointing at the bird perched just below her bedroom window. His rustic feathers glint shades of red and copper in the morning sunlight as he swivels and cocks his head her way. "Even you, Reginald, with your get me up attitude, cannot dampen my mood today. Today is day two of my show and yesterday Amber rocked it!"

Heading to the shed, she pulls out the food and sprinkles it on the ground, watching the hens swarm around her feet. Smiling, she skips to the barn to feed Pinecone, watching her slip in with her namesake in her mouth. "Silly kitty. I have food for you." Poppy drops a scoopful in the dish and checks the water bowl, rinsing and refilling it, along with the outside chicken one. Once her farm chores are done, including her daily call, she heads in for her coffee, pouring it into a cup and carrying it back to her room.

Setting it down, she boots her laptop up and spends the day watching and following the show, she sketches out ideas as other designs walk the runway, and how she would change or modify it to make it hers. She flips through the growing comments, responding when she needs to and doing everything that she can behind the scenes.

At the end of the day, she jumps from her seat in delight, seeing three of her designs on the large screen behind the announcers going over the event standings. "YES! Those are mine! Oh, my gawd! They picked mine!" Excitement and sadness fills her with her success, both that they chose her designs and that her Grams was not here to see it.

Needing to talk to someone, she flips to a new tab, and video calls her friend, mentally yelling at her to pick up. Delight fills her at her friend's matching smile. "Amber! Did you see that?!"

"I did! Congratulations!"

"Thank you. It's because of you that my designs were even modeled."

"No problem! I am glad three of your designs made it."

"I saw at least one of yours up there too!"

"Yes, I had two make it, which I am super happy with. We did it Poppy! Now we just need to keep it up."

"I will! I already have ideas in my sketchbook. Obviously I really wanted to be at the fashion show, but a part of me was looking forward to the fabric show-and-tell more. Pick me out some good fabrics for dresses; ones that would work for flowing skirts and perhaps even peasant style sleeves."

"Got it. What's your budget?" Amber asks.

"Right now, somewhat limited. But in five weeks, I will have more options. I just need ideas of what's new that I can work with."

"How about I take videos of the way the fabric hangs and flows, then get cards from all the sellers so you can contact them later?"

"Perfect."

"Alright Pops, I gotta get to the largest fashion after-party there is. Perhaps I will find myself some hot hookup!"

Poppy rolls her eyes and laughs at her friend, knowing her penchant for finding a man with the same interests as her. "You know he won't be in our industry, Amber. You need to branch out of fashion for that. Perhaps the hotel manager where they are holding the show or a limo driver?"

"What are you saying?"

"I am saying that most of the men are spoken for and they don't play in our field."

"Whatever. They can't all bat for the other team and I am going to find the one that doesn't."

"Good luck with that. Thanks again Amber."

"You're welcome Pops! Talk to you later!"

Poppy ends the video call, flipping back to the organizers of the event, her eyes drifting over to her designs once more. She presses the screenshot button and saves the image before closing her computer down. Her eyes glance to the clock, seeing it flash 9:18, knowing she should be crashing, but finding too much pent up energy.

Running down the stairs, she heads outside, dancing in the setting sun and the cooling air. She finds a grassy spot and lies down, staring into the sky, watching as the stars wink into existence when night falls, something she rarely has time for in the city, if you could even see the stars past the streetlights and smog. An hour later, she rises and brushes the grass off her clothes. Heading inside, she locks the house up and crashes.

Sunday morning, Poppy rolls over in the bed, feeling the cozy warmth of the blankets cocooning her, with the happy bliss still radiating from the show. She sighs softly as Reginald's voice breaks the silence of the room. Closing her eyes, she draws in a deep breath, wondering how Grams could have enjoyed having that racket wake her every morning.

Pushing herself out of bed with a groan, she pads to the bathroom, and steps into the shower, letting the hot water drive the stiffness out of her shoulders from all the haying and then sitting at the computer for hours on end. Twenty minutes later, she steps outside into the morning sun, coffee in hand. After feeding the chickens and Pinecone, she sits down on the back porch, watching them scratch around in the dirt and listening to their quiet clucks of contentment.

Sipping her coffee, she lifts her gaze to the rooster sitting on the shed, protecting his flock. "Now, why can't you be as peaceful as them? Huh? Would it kill you to lower your tone, just a smidge, so that those of us that don't care to wake up bright and early can sleep in?" She watches him tilt his head at her words, as if trying to comprehend them. "Right, way to go Poppy. Talking to the bloody cock and hoping he understands. You really are losing it."

Finishing her coffee, she rises and heads inside, checking the clock, knowing that Astrid is coming by in a few hours to get her hay. Finding herself at a loss for what to do, she sets about cleaning the house and washing her clothes and bedding, hanging them out on the line to dry just as a vehicle pulls up into her driveway. Rounding the house, she spots an older woman clambering out of a beat-up pickup truck that's seen better days, wearing blue overalls and a grey shirt, with her hair tied back in a ponytail. Glasses rest on the bridge of her nose, enhancing her grey eyes, ones she vaguely recognizes from her childhood. "Hello?"

"Poppy?"

"Yes, that's me."

"I'm Astrid. I am here for the hay. You were expecting me?"

"Right, yes. Is it eleven already? Shoot, sorry. I got caught up in cleaning."

"That's easy to do. Did you want me to back the truck up to the barn?"

"Umm. Sure. I haven't done this, so I am unfamiliar with the routine. I just found Gram's list on her computer, so I know who the hay belongs to."

Astrid chuckles. "Well, it belongs to you at the moment, at least until you make us pay, because if her other clients are like me, she collects upon pickup."

"Right, that could be a problem. I didn't find any prices."

"Good thing you called me first, then. Hay normally goes for about ten dollars a bale, but Rose charges fourteen."

"Why so much more?"

"Because her hay is far superior to any other hay out there. The horses eat less and it seems to give their coats a shine I have not seen with other hay. It's worth the price."

"I see."

"Trust me. The others will say the same thing. Now, if you want to open the barn doors, I can back my truck right up to it. There is a lift in the barn that she sets against the tailgate. It helps us get the hay into the truck. Normally I take about sixteen bales at a time, and keep the rest here for storage."

"Yes, I saw that. Grams has numbered the stalls and assigned one to each person on her spreadsheet."

"If you are good with that, I would like to keep the same deal I had with your Grams."

"I will…" Poppy stops, knowing she probably should not be telling them she plans on selling the farm until it's actually up for sale. "Sure. That's fine with me. I will see if I can find that lift."

"Great."

Poppy runs to the barn doors and opens them wide as Astrid hops back in her truck and backs it up. She scans the stalls quickly, heading to the back where all her tools are. Finding what she figures is the lift, she pulls it out and rolls it towards the truck.

"That's it."

"I hope you know how to work it."

"I do." She takes the lift from her and slides it up to the truck, adjusting it to sit wide side parallel with it. "Now we stack it four bales high. It does five, but I am not that tall." Astrid leads Poppy into her stall, where they each grab a bale and half carry, half drag it back, setting them on the lift and repeating the process. Astrid leads her over to the controls. "It operates on a car battery, so you will probably need to check it from time to time. This switch unlocks it so the lift can move. This button turns it on and this one raises and lowers, depending on which way the switch is. Up is up and, well, down is down." She flips the switch up and watches as it rises, stopping it when it's level with the truck. "Now, I will drag the bale onto the truck and you raise it so the next one is level. Got it?"

Poppy grins. "Got it! This is far easier than chucking them into the back of a truck, like I saw them do when I was growing up."

"Yes, it is. I think Rose purchased it about three years ago. It's a lifesaver. I have one for offloading, too." Astrid climbs up into the back of the truck and slides the top bale off, pushing it up against the cab. "Alright, next one." She waits as Poppy lifts it and repeats the process.

Forty-five minutes later, Poppy helps Astrid strap the hay down, feeling pride in their accomplishment. "How long does this last?"

"A couple of months, but I supplement by letting them graze and adding oats to their diet."

"So, is there enough to get you through the winter?"

"Yes, unless they suddenly start eating more, it should be enough."

"Good. I think I will have a few extra bales if you do."

"Rose usually does. Others might need it though, so promise it to no one until they actually run out."

"Understood."

Once the hay is secure, Astrid walks to the cab and opens the door. She pulls out an envelope and hands it over to Poppy. "This covers all the hay, plus storage for the winter."

Poppy accepts it and opens it, her eyes widening at the price on the check. "Are you sure?"

"It's what I paid Rose every year. She really needs to raise her storage prices, though. Other barns might be cheaper in hay, but they are double and triple her storage fees."

"Thank you! I will keep that in mind."

"It was nice to see you again, Poppy. Don't clean too much."

"I won't. I was nearly done."

Astrid hops in her truck and rolls the window down. "Good. Now, I know you have only been back for about a week, but Sundays are rest days around here. The library has a projector and plays older movies for free for the locals to watch. You put in your requests and they pick from them. I know it's not like the big city and going to a new release at the theatre, but people love it. There is an all you can eat buffet at the Country Shack Bar and Grill Sunday nights. It's also the local hangout for kids in your age bracket. Of course there is the market during the week, that I am sure you know of. On the main board in town, there are also horse rentals if you want to go for a ride through the countryside."

"Thanks, but I am more of an indoor girl. Give me a sewing machine and fabric and I will hibernate for days, crafting."

"There is a local fabric shop, the Cloth Depot. I believe it's a lot of quilting stuff, but upstairs, they have more extravagant fabrics. Usually for costume designs and such, but talk to Barb. She can bring some in. I think you can even rent her machines at the back of the shop."

Poppy's eyes light up at the thought. "I might just have to stop by tomorrow. Thank you."

"You're welcome. See you later Poppy."

"Bye!" Poppy waves to her, watching as she drives away. Pushing the lifter back to where she found it, she closes up the barn and heads inside, her thoughts swirling at visiting the bank, the lawyer, and then the fabric shop tomorrow after the market, especially the money from the check burning a hole in her hot little hands.

Cockery Delight

Monday morning, Poppy sits in her booth, watching as people move through the aisles, pausing to look over the wares, with a lot stopping to talk to her about her Grams. She feels a weariness creeping in, knowing she could not do this daily like the others. Feeling a hand on her shoulder, she jumps, her eyes lifting to meet Clara's.

"You're zoning Poppy."

"Yes. I was thinking about how Grams did this. There is no way I could do this daily."

"Grams loved this, but you are not her. She also didn't have her death looming over her like you do and everyone that stops to talk reminds you of the fact." Clara sits on the chair beside her. "Personally, I think you are out here too soon. You should have waited a month."

"Yah, I might go back to painting. I just thought I would get Gram's pottery out here."

"Are you selling a lot?"

"I am actually, everyone wants a piece, knowing that no more is being made."

"That's good. I can cover your booth if you want to stretch."

"Thanks. I might do that." Poppy rises to her feet and rolls her shoulders back, her eyes darting momentarily over to Rowan's booth, before snapping back at the grating voice of Melody. Muttering under her breath to Clara. "And here I was, hoping she might actually have a job and not be here."

Clara chuckles. "She does. It's called the town tramp and the hours are eight in the evening till three in the morning."

"That's evil!" Poppy coughs at her words, straightening as Melody stops in front of her booth.

"Oh, look. It's the wannabe fashion designer, resorting to selling cheap pottery just to scrape by." Melody picks up a plate and turns it over in her hands before letting it slip from her fingers. It crashes to the ground, shattering at her feet. "Oops."

Poppy gasps at the disrespect and the broken plate, something that is irreplaceable, before glaring at Melody, tuning out the rest of the crowd. "What the fuck, Melody? Grams made that."

"Do I look like I care?"

Clara rounds the stall and places her hands on her hips. "You cow! You did that deliberately, so you better pay for that."

Poppy narrows her eyes and places a hand on Clara's arm, squatting down to pick up the pieces of the plate. "It's alright Clara. Melody can't afford to buy Grams's plate. It's out of her price range."

Melody gasps in anger. "Excuse me Bitch?"

"Well, I mean it's obvious. Just look at what you are wearing." Poppy straightens and places the broken shards on another plate in her booth. Turning her attention back to Melody, her eyes sweep down over the sleek, cream jumpsuit, its structured shoulders and cinched waist circled with a brown leather belt, screaming runway, but she knows better. The oversized sunglasses and designer clutch dangling in one hand, each out of place for this town, giving off the compensation for inadequacy vibes. Her gaze lingers on the gold-tipped stilettos, knowing they are the worst footwear for the uneven market grounds.

"I will have you know…" She waves a hand at herself. "This is Jean-Pierre Coq original."

"Yes, it's Jean-Pierre Coq clothing, but it's last year's style and his bargain basement design. The ones he makes to sell in the cheap-marts and discount stores for those that can't afford the real thing. Even I designed some for my fashion show this past weekend." Poppy lifts her hand to stop Melody from talking. "Uh ah. I'm not done. Any designer, who is anyone, knows you design for three levels of classes. The high-end one, with the most expensive fabrics; ones that you can bend, pleat, tuck and twist to get the desired look. Then there's the mid class, where the fabrics are cheaper. They don't flow as well, so you make adjustments, subtle, but it's there. Finally, what you are wearing right now. The low end designs. The fabrics are cheap and unforgiving, so you really have to adjust the pattern to make them stylish. A trained designer can see the immediate tells of the way the outfit is made. It is, after all, the first thing they teach us in design school. And yours, my dear Melody, screams of cheap, trying to be more than it is."

Clara smothers the laughter escaping from her at Poppy's words, unlike the populace around, who start snickering at Melody standing there.

Melody's eyes narrow as she glares at Poppy, digging in her designer clutch and pulling out some cash. She slaps it on the table, hissing in anger. "There, you stupid bitch, I have cash." With that, she turns and strides away.

Poppy watches her walk away stiffly, the heels sinking in the dirt, causing it to be more of a stagger than a prideful walk. She glances over at the broken plate and calls after her. "You forgot your purchase! I can package it up for you!"

"Whatever!"

When Melody disappears, Poppy realizes that the people in the surrounding stalls are clapping. A blush stains her cheeks and she ducks back behind her booth, feeling Clara settle in beside her. "Well, that was embarrassing."

"Nah, that was perfect, and everyone loved the show."

"Right."

"You just wait. I bet your business picks up." She leans in and whispers. "Even Rowan over there is looking at you like you're his next hit."

Poppy glances over to Rowan, feeling a sudden heat fill her at his smoldering look. She shifts in the chair, feeling his desire sweep through her and matching it in spades. "Clara! That is not true." She hisses softly, avoiding looking Rowan's way in case he knows they are talking about him.

"Well, your name is a flower that does have an opioid made of it. It makes sense."

"It doesn't matter. I am not a drug..."

Clara leans in and whispers in her ear. "I bet he could give you a high! Especially since he's coming over."

"What?" Her eyes lift and lock onto Rowans, finding herself instantly lost in the depths of his green eyes, watching the way his pupils dilate as they look over her. "Rowan."

"Poppy. I watched your minor altercation. I think it deserves a coffee and since I am getting one for myself, did you want one?"

"Sure, that would be great."

"Watch my booth while I am gone?" He asks.

"Of course." She watches him disappear into the crowds, heading toward the food trucks located in the far corner of the market.

"Yes, a drug, for sure." Clara laughs, nudging Poppy to draw her back to the customer that approached the stall. "Earth to Poppy. You have a customer."

Poppy snaps her gaze to Clara in confusion, following her nod and turning to the customer standing before her. "Sorry, I was distracted. How can I help you?"

The woman smiles, winking her way. "That young man is a fine distraction."

"Yes, he is. Wait." She stops the lady from grabbing a plate. "There was an incident earlier. Let me remove the broken one first." Poppy mumbles and grabs the dish with the broken pottery, pouring the fragments into a bag. Grabbing a cloth, she wipes the plate clean and places it back. "Alright. I don't want anyone getting cut on my first day selling in the market."

"I saw. Did you make these?"

"No, my Grams made them before she passed away. So what you see is what I have."

"Well, the details of the rooster are quite stunning, especially the way she has him standing at attention on this set. I would like all four plates and the two bowls, if I may."

Poppy covers her mouth as a giggle escapes her. "Thank you."

"Did I miss something?"

"No.. Yes... Grams clearly modeled her designs off her rooster Reginald on the farm, and I've been calling him the damn cock."

The woman laughs, recalling what she said. "I understand. Now then, can you please wrap my attentive cocks up?"

Clara bursts out in laughter and falls off the chair, clutching at her stomach. "Of course she can. Would you like them handled with care, or do you prefer them nice and snug?"

"Clara!! I always handle them with care!!!" Poppy tries to send a stern look before breaking into laughter too. "Besides, its more like, would you like them double-wrapped for extra protection?"

The woman joins them with a chuckle, along with a few others listening to the conversation. "Well, I wouldn't want any unexpected surprises. Best make it double; safety first, after all."

"Got it!" Poppy double wraps each plate carefully, tucking them into one of the cloth bags she found in the bins. Handing them over and accepting the money, she smiles. "Here they are, an adorable bundle of cocks."

"Why thank you. This adventure is definitely getting posted on social media, letting my friends and followers know that you have the best cocks in the country."

"I appreciate it. Please inform them that each one is different in shape and size... Oh, and that they are limited editions."

"I bet. With cocks like these, you are going to sell out fast. I do hope you can learn to handle pottery as well as your Grams did. I would hate for others to miss out on this experience."

"I don't know. I am not as skilled with my hands."

Clara pauses in her laughter. "Yes, you are. You just have a different skill with them. You work better with the wrappings!"

"Clara!"

"Wrappings?"

"I am a fashion designer. I just launched my debut line this weekend."

"Interesting, I will have look that up, too. What name should I be looking for?"

"Poppy McInnes."

"Thank you." The woman grins, looping the bag over her arm and tucking it against her chest. "Well, I must say, this has been the most… satisfying shopping experience I've had in a while."

Clara grins. "Poppy aims to please."

Poppy shakes her head with a laugh. "And to make sure everyone leaves happy and well-handled."

The woman chuckles. "Oh, I'll definitely be coming again."

Clara gasps at her scandalous words. "Ma'am, at least take her out to dinner first."

The area erupts into laughter, Poppy's laugh catches in her throat as her eyes land on Rowans, standing there, holding two cups of coffee. Laughter dancing in his eyes and a smirk on his lips.

"Have a good day." The woman's eyes roam over the pair with a knowing look. She sends a wink Poppy's way and wanders off, leaving them to talk.

Rowan steps forward and hands over the cup of coffee, brushing her fingers gently. "Seems like you are fitting into the market pretty well."

"I am. Thank you."

Clara pushes up on her elbows to scowl at Rowan. "Wait. You got her a coffee and not me! I am crushed!"

Rowan looks down at the coffee remaining in his hands and places it on the back side of the table. "Here, you can have mine."

Poppy shakes her head. "No. Clara and I can share. She's just harassing you."

"You guys are hilarious. If I hadn't seen you slam Melody, I would say you are too nice for your own good Pops." Clara laughs and stands up, brushing the dirt and grass off her clothes. "You keep your coffee Rowan.

I already had mine this morning. Too many of those, and I am flying high. It's a drug, just like my girl here."

"Clara! Don't you have someplace to be?"

"Nope! Not until later." She smiles. "Right now, my job today is to pester you."

"Well, you are succeeding."

Rowan chuckles and collects his coffee. "Well, thank you Clara for not desiring to take away my addiction." Turning back to Poppy, he smiles. "Thank you for looking after my booth. Perhaps with this success, we will see you here a few days a week."

"Only until the pottery runs out."

"Unless, of course, you try your hand at it."

Poppy shakes her head. "Nope, I don't think so."

Rowan reaches out to take her free hand, turning it over in his palm, his fingers caressing hers gently. His eyes darken in desire as he lifts his gaze to her. "You have soft hands, despite baling hay the past week. I guarantee these hands could master anything you wanted them to." He brings them up to his lips and kisses the back of them, his eyes never leaving hers. "I see people at my booth, so I should get back to it." Releasing her hand, he winks and heads over to his booth, settling behind it and turning his attention over to the customer.

Poppy blushes, her gaze dropping to her hand as she turns it over, still feeling the burn of his lips upon it.

"See, I told ya. Even I felt that sizzle."

Poppy sighs, bringing the coffee up to her lips to gulp it down. "Yes, and what do I do about it in five weeks, Clara?"

"I don't know, but at least you have some time to figure it out. Go with the flow."

"I suppose." Poppy turns her attention back to the customers arriving at her stall, talking to them and selling her wares with the help of Clara until she has to leave for work. At the end of the market, Poppy packs up with much less merchandise, thanks to a lot of the locals wanting a piece of Gram's pottery to remember her by. She loads the now lighter bins into the wagon and ensures her stall is left clean. Tugging it over to Rowan's booth, she stops and watches him. "Did you need a hand?"

"Nope, I got this down."

"Alright. Thanks again for the coffee."

"You're welcome. Am I coming by in a few hours?"

"Sure. That sounds good."

Rowan straightens and faces her, noticing the differences from even a week ago. Her sun kissed skin only complimented the brightness in her eyes and the smile that graced her lips more often. "Do you want help getting that to the truck?"

"Nah, it's much lighter. I can probably combine it into one bin next time. I will see you later."

"Yes, you will."

Poppy weaves her wagon through the aisles as others pack up to go, with a few customers trying for last-minute deals. At her truck, she loads the bins and the wagon into the back and pulls out her keys. Hopping in, she starts it, and shifts it into gear. A tap on her window draws her attention as she drops her foot on the brake and rolls it down. "Josh?"

"I just want to say, you don't need to call today since I saw you vending."

"Thanks. I will probably stop by next week with receipts. I made enough today to buy more stuff."

"How's the house coming along?"

"I've painted a few rooms, and I got one order of hay gone with a second in progress. Still working on the remaining, but it's getting there."

"Good to hear. I won't keep you. Take care Poppy."

"I will. Thanks." Poppy turns the steering wheel and drives away, glancing in the rearview mirror, seeing Josh and Rowan talking together, finding herself curious as to about what. Twenty minutes later, she parks the truck in the garage and unloads the pottery into a corner. Grabbing her riches, she heads inside to count it and make lunch. Finding herself looking forward to baling hay and spending time with Rowan this afternoon without people milling around them.

Hours later, dressed in jeans and a tank top, she is back out in the hayfields with Rowan, working on baling her next order. As they near the cornfield, she pauses raking, her eyes glancing over the rows of stalks, noticing how much greener they are then even a week ago. "Do you see that, Rowan?"

"See what?" He stops the tractor and lifts his gaze in the direction she's looking.

"I don't know. The corn stalks seem greener, like fuller."

"Well, it is getting close to harvesting time. They will fill out."

Poppy chews on her lower lip, contemplating his words. "I suppose. I just always remember the stalks having more of a gold tinge to them. Even from last week, these seem healthier."

"Not sure what to tell you. They look fine to me. We will tackle those fields in a few weeks."

Staring at the fields a moment longer, she turns back to the hay behind the tractor, and sets about fluffing it out to dry properly. Hours later, the pair of them are trekking back to the house where Poppy bids him farewell for the night, despite wanting to invite him in. After dinner, she heads out to the back porch and sits down with a cup of tea, watching the sunset upon the farm.

The next eleven days slip by as she settles into a routine; waking up each morning to her overly enthusiastic cock, crowing impatiently until she satisfies him and his harem of hens with breakfast. With that royal duty handled, she heads to the barn to feed Pinecone before finally making her own breakfast. Once that's complete, she checks in with her daily call to the lawyer's office and spends the morning painting. She spends her afternoons in the fields with Rowan, where laughter and easy camaraderie make the work almost enjoyable.

Hen Party

September 4

On Friday afternoon, Poppy turns to Rowan. "Do you know if they run the market on Labor day?"

"No, it's a day off for everyone. All the shops will close too, so get what you need beforehand."

Poppy nods. "I figured. Then, I will see you Tuesday at the market instead."

"I will be there. Did you need any weekend help?"

"No, not this one. I have a sleepover planned."

Rowan arches a brow, feeling a hint of jealousy brewing inside him as his hands clench in his pockets. "A sleepover?"

"Yes, with Amber, my college bestie and Clara, who you know, my high school bestie. They are arriving tomorrow sometime, probably just after lunch and staying till Sunday afternoon, maybe even Monday."

Rowan chuckles. "Ah, so the hens are gathering in the henhouse! Let me guess, there'll be clucking, gossip, and maybe a few feathers ruffling? Should I be worried?"

Poppy smirks and crosses her arms as she tilts her head at him. "Oh, absolutely. We'll be plotting world domination between face masks, movies and wine." She pauses, eyes glinting with mischief. "Or at the very least, deciding which poor soul to hex for bad ex-boyfriend behavior. I think Clara's has a strong lead in that department." She leans in slightly, lowering her voice conspiratorially and teasing him gently. "You're safe... for now. Unless, of course, you do something to ruffle my feathers."

"Well, as long as you don't turn the henhouse into a full-blown pecking party, I suppose I'll survive. Should I warn the neighbors?"

Poppy grins, tapping a finger against her chin in mock consideration. "Hmm, that depends… Do they scare easily? Because once the wine starts flowing, there's no telling if we'll be cackling like hens or summoning spirits." She leans in just a little, her voice dropping to a whisper. "If you hear eerie chanting at midnight, just go back to sleep. No need to investigate. Unless, of course, you want to join the hen party. I mean, we could always use a sacrificial rooster."

Laughter escapes him. "Well then. Thank you for the warning. Ebonwind and I will be certain to steer clear of your property for the next two days. Perhaps I will take Reginald with me just to keep him safe. Us roosters, we need to stick together."

Unable to contain it any longer, Poppy breaks into laughter. "The cock is safe for the weekend. Clara's bringing pizza. Now, next weekend though, his luck might run out."

Rowan chuckles, reaching up to brush some strands of hair off her face. "All humor aside. Have a great time with the girls."

She tilts her head and leans into his touch. "I will. Thank you."

Rowan turns and walks down the front steps. At the bottom, he stops and glances back. "Hey, I know you haven't mentioned it, but the Harvest Moon Festival is coming up on the nineteenth. Would you be willing to go with me?"

"As in a date?"

Rowan tilts his head. "Yes… as in a date. We could do dinner first, then walk around town."

Poppy ponders him for a moment. "Sure, but I owe Clara a hayride. I already promised her."

"Ooh, Ouch, choosing a hen over a rooster!"

Poppy laughs, a gentle teasing lacing her voice. "That's right. She's known me longer, so she has seniority when it comes to rolling in the hay!"

He chuckles, arching a brow at her comment. "Alright then, I can part with you for one ride. After that, you are mine to roll on the hay with."

"Deal." A soft blush crosses her cheeks as her thoughts drift to a different sort of rolling in the hay. Drawing from her thoughts, she watches him get into the truck and drive away. Closing the door, she wanders back to the living room, recalling the sleepovers they had as kids. Walking down the hall, she peeks in the spare room that was always a storage space and spies the two mattresses propped up against the wall. "Score. Grams. You are the best pack rat ever."

Moving back to the living room, she sets about moving the furniture around, clearing a space in the middle, trying to recall how her Grams had done it. An hour later, happy with her progress, she stares at the two double mattresses lying in the center of the room. Heading into the linen closet, she pulls out the bedding and covers them, dropping the extra pillows on top. Placing her hands on her hips, she grins. "All set for tomorrow." Padding back to the kitchen, she makes some dinner and heads upstairs to retire for the evening with a good book and a long soak.

Saturday morning, Poppy rolls out of bed, just as the yodeling of the rooster filters in through her open bedroom window. Leaning outside, she glares at the bird. "Haven't you learned by now, you bloody bird, that you are working with a city girl who likes to sleep in? I will feed you when I feed you!" She ducks back inside, glancing at the clock, seeing 6:10 am flashing at her.

Muttering under her breath at the fact that he's getting earlier every day, she stomps downstairs to the back door. Flinging it open, she steps into the warm air, knowing today was going to be another scorcher. After feeding the chickens, she wanders back to the henhouse. Spending some time examining the eggs with the lightbox she found tucked away in the corner, she marks the ones with a felt marker that she'd found dark spots in. A small measure of excitement filling her at the thought of having fresh eggs for breakfast now that she has Googled how to check for embryos.

She grins as the orange tabby bounds out of the forest, tail high and triumphant, a fresh treasure clutched in her jaws, watching her slip through the barn's cat door. Making her way to the barn, she opens the large door and steps into the shadowed interior. The familiar scent of hay and wood greets her, along with the sight of Pinecones ever-growing hoard; twice the size it was when she arrived three weeks ago. "Well, Pinecone, I see now why Grams cleared out your stash. If you keep this up, I might have to stage my own little heist."

Scooping the cat up, she carries her to the worktable and sets her down, chuckling as Pinecone expertly weaves between buckets, eyes locked on her as if willing the kibble to appear faster. Reaching out, she scratches her under her chin. "At least you're not as obnoxious as the cock out there, pussy cat. He struts around like he owns the place, screaming for my attention at ungodly hours. Meanwhile, you just lurk in the shadows, stealing pinecones and waiting for snacks and cuddles. My type of pet." She opens the bucket and drops some kibble in the bowl. Giving her one last pat, she heads back into the house to eat, make her call, and prepare for her friends.

Just after lunch, the sound of a car draws her attention. Poppy runs to the door and opens it, a wide smile crossing her lips at her friend pulling into the driveway. When she gets out and approaches, Poppy launches forward and wraps her arms around Amber, crushing her in a hug. "Amber. It feels like it's been forever." She steps back and looks over at her friend, smiling at the fact that she adorned her lashes with red mascara. "Wow, you look great!"

"And you look like a farm girl! What is that? A t-shirt and shorts? Man, you need to show your legs more gurl! They are fabulous. Had I known you were hiding those beneath your clothes, I would have had you model my clothes. No more pants for you!"

Poppy laughs. "Yes, I will admit, I didn't bring enough clothes for six weeks and Grams stocked the closet with jeans, shorts and T's, so this is what you get. Besides, you make men's clothes!"

"Yes, well, that's because my brother volunteered to be a model. You are being volun'told now. Besides, this look, it actually kind of suits you."

"Gurl," Poppy mimics her slur. "It sooo does not, but it works for the farm. Come on in. Clara is on her way. She just called. The pizza is running a little late."

"Yes!" Amber walks into the living room, seeing all the furniture pushed to the side and two mattresses on the floor with bedding spread across it. "Oh, my gawd. A real life slumber party!" She drops her small bag on the floor, kicks off her shoes and jumps on the beds, settling in.

"Yes. Grams had them for us when I was growing up. They were still in the spare room, so I rearranged the living room for us." She looks critically at Amber's designer clothes. "Although you might want to change into something more comfortable."

"I have Pjs! Where's the bathroom?"

"Back in the hall. The first door, right after the stairs."

"I brought the booze and a few movies to add to our selection." Amber clambers off the bed and grabs her bag, pulling out the wine and handing it over.

"Perfect. I'll throw it in the fridge to chill." She pads to the kitchen and returns moments later to the sound of car tires on the gravel. Heading to the door, she can hear Amber vacating the bathroom behind her. Poppy leans in the doorway, watching Clara park the car and hop out, three large pizza boxes in hand.

"Ooh, has the pizza arrived?" Amber asks.

"It has, and with it, my high school bestie. Three pizzas?"

Clara chuckles. "Yes! Lunch, dinner and breakfast in the morning. I wanted to make sure we had enough."

Amber steps aside as Clara enters the house. "Right on, so the college and high school besties finally get to meet! Hi! I'm Amber."

Clara hands the pizza over to Poppy and turns to Amber, shaking the hand offered. "I'm Clara!" Her eyes drift to the mattresses. "Wow, Poppy!

When you invited us to stay, I assumed we would be in the guest rooms, not the actual sleepover room. You are the best!"

Poppy eyes the boxes, then nods. "Well. There's only one actual guest room now. It seems that Grams turned the one off the kitchen into an office." She gestures toward a nearby door. "That one under the stairs, so to speak, is still the storage room where I found the mattresses. Which leaves the two rooms upstairs; mine and hers. And I'm not sleeping in hers. Hell, the only time I even step foot in there is to use the soaker tub, and even then, I feel like I'm trespassing." She shrugs with a small grin. "Besides, I thought roughing it like we did when we were kids would be fun."

"Right on! I need to grab my overnight bag. I want to get into pajamas, too. I can't remember the last time I lounged around like this. Well I can, but we are not going there." Clara races back outside to her car, and pops the trunk, pulling out a large suitcase. She drags it back across the gravel and up the porch.

Poppy eyes it warily. "Are you moving in?"

Clara laughs. "Nah, this is all that we need for a slumber party. My clothes, and lots of snacks!" She drags it into the living room and unzips it, pulling out a small satchel of clothes tucked between boxes of cookies, bags of chips, packages of licorice and other goodies.

Poppy laughs at all the snacks they munched on as kids. "What, no ice cream?"

"Nah, I figured you would have that."

Carrying the pizza to the kitchen, she places it on the table. "You're right. I do. Chocolate, butterscotch, and vanilla. Alright, Ambers already beat us, so let's get changed and start the party!" Twenty minutes later, the three of them are curled up with their pizza, wine and movies playing on the TV, laughing and conversing as if they had all known each other since childhood, staying up well into the evening.

The next morning, the three of them groan in dismay at the rooster yodeling outside, reminding Poppy that she forgot to warn her friends about that. She mutters softly and rolls over, pulling the blanket over her head. "Rise and shine! My cock's always up early."

Clara giggles at her grumpiness. "I see Poppy still handles mornings like a champ. Cock-a-doodle-do and all."

Amber snickers. "Oh, so we are going there, are we? Let's see. He may be a farm boy, but he knows how to handle his cock."

Poppy snorts at their comments and flips the covers back off to scowl at them. "You guys are bad. Why did I even invite you here?"

"Because you love us! Now, keep it going."

"Fine." She tilts her head as she ponders it, tapping her lips with her finger. "Gotta keep my cock under control. I don't need it causing a scene."

"That's because he's up at the crack of dawn, ready to go." Clara rolls over in laughter. "Or, better yet, you can't keep a good cock down. It's always standing tall and proud."

Amber laughs with Clara. "Alright, here's one. They say a firm grip on your cock is key to keeping it in line, especially in the morning." Her gaze shifts over to Poppy. "Speaking of which, have you had the chance to feel up your boy's toys yet?"

Poppy blushes. "No! Amber!!"

Clara stops and pushes herself up to look Poppy over as well. "Wait, Boy's toy? Did you make it past first base with Rowan and not tell me?"

Amber smirks. "With a kiss like she described, the hen can't resist a cock with confidence."

Poppy tosses a pillow at them, laughter dancing in her eyes. "I am not a hen, but every farm needs a strong cock to keep things in order." Turning to Clara. "And No!! It's kinda hot and cold right now. He's difficult."

"When it's hot, it's roasting." Amber replies. "Nothing gets the ladies clucking like a big, proud cock."

Clara laughs. "That's so true!! You should hear the gossip at the market."

Poppy groans and grabs Clara's pillow, smacking her in the head with it. "Oh, I have. Remember, I've been selling there."

Clara collapses back down on the bed, yanking the pillow out of Poppy's hands. "Careful, He's got quite the pecking order, if you know what I mean and struts around like he owns the henhouse."

"Gawd! If I had more pillows, I would toss them at you both. You are awful!"

Clara tosses her pillow back. "Seriously though. How are you two? The sizzle is there. Everyone can see it. The evil side of me loves that Melody is seething inside and that you slammed her hard that first Monday."

Poppy sighs, her fingers caressing the pillow. "I don't know. Like I said, one moment I feel like I will burn to a crisp beneath his gaze, then the next minute, he's withdrawn and pulling away and I am left standing alone on the frozen tundra. When he steals a kiss from me, my toes curl and my core fills with flames, crying out for his touch. It makes me want more, but then my logical brain says no, you are leaving. He's a farm boy and will stay because he loves it here. That much is clear."

"Have you talked to him about it?"

"No… And honestly, I don't know if I want to. I mean, I am only planning to be here six weeks. Talking to him means commitment and if I do that, I might have to admit to myself that I like it here. That I like him enough to stay. Then where does that leave me with all my schooling and the fashion industry I have been trying to succeed in? I mean, even that bloody cock is growing on me and I don't want to like that."

"That's rough, but I think you need to talk to him sooner rather than later. You are both getting attached to each other, that much is clear. As for your fashion. Do it here. Then make weekend trips if you need it."

"Or I can help, like I did for the World Fashion Day show." Amber pouts, tugging at the blankets. "It's totally unfair that you both have seen this hunk, and I haven't."

Poppy's eyes light up as she looks over at the clock on the wall. "Well, if we get our asses in gear, we might catch him riding along the creek's edge near the tire swing."

Amber perks up at her words. "Wait, he rides and you have a tire swing?"

"Yes. My parents had some people help put it up when I was a kid just before they passed. It's one of the farm's old tractor tires."

"So we can fit in it?"

"Yes."

"Well, why are we not out there playing?!"

"Coffee and breakfast first!"

"Deal."

An hour later, the three of them are dancing across the fields with their arms full of picnic gear, heading to the cluster of willow trees lining the creek where the swing waits. Crows caw in the sky above them, swooping along the wind, mimicking their happiness.

As they step beneath the vines dangling around them, Amber gasps in delight. "WOW! I would become a farm girl for this!" She races over to the tire and clambers in. Kicking her feet back and letting it swing. "I am so jealous that you guys grew up with this. We lived in the city with no trees. All I had was a measly swing set. One that you didn't dare test for fear it would collapse on you."

Poppy laughs and spreads a blanket out on the moss. She drops the cooler containing sodas, leftover pizza and sandwiches in it, and settles on the blanket, watching her friend on the tire. "There were swing sets at the school, but this is way better."

"I'll say. Two of us can fit in here easily."

Clara runs over and pushes the tire, forcing it to swing wildly. "Three actually. Two inside the tire and one on top."

"Ooh, so you have tried it before."

Poppy laughs, "Hey, we have tried seven or eight before."

Clara giggles. "I think the max we got in was eight, but we were much smaller than we are now."

"I would have loved this as a kid." Amber smiles wistfully.

"Until the twist and spin of death."

"What is that?"

"Clara and I will show you." Poppy rises and runs over to the tire, winking at Clara as she takes a side. The pair of them walked around in a circle, twisting and tightening the rope above them. Once they are certain it's enough, they push it back as far as they can, and let go, watching the tire spin rapidly while swinging, hearing Amber's scream of delight. Shortly after, pounding hooves fill the air as all three girls look in his direction, seeing a panicked Rowan riding across the stream towards them.

Poppy smiles up at him. "Rowan, what are you doing here?"

His eyes quickly access the three women, two standing back and the one still spinning in the tire, desperately clinging on for dear life. "I heard a scream."

Poppy snickers. "Yes, that was Amber experiencing the spin of death on the tire."

"She seems to be still alive and barely kicking."

"Yes. Well, she has a better grip on the rubber than we expected."

Rowan chuckles and slides off Ebonwind, stepping closer to them. "Good to know she's got a firm grasp on protection."

Amber rests her chin on the tire as the tire slows to a reasonable speed. "Even I know a strong grip is important… wouldn't want things getting out of hand."

Clara bursts out laughing. "OMG, this has been the best weekend of puns ever. Are you saying it's got a little too much bounce for your liking?"

Poppy slaps her shoulder. "Clara!!"

Rowan chuckles, arching a brow as his gaze lands on Poppy. "Hey, as long as she knows how to handle rubber under pressure, she'll be just fine."

Amber groans at the terrible puns, her eyes sweeping up and down Rowan, following his gaze to her friend and feeling the sexual tension in the air between them. "Oh, I definitely do, but clearly, I'm not your preferred ride."

Poppy gasps, a blush staining her cheeks. "Amber!"

Clara howls with laughter, clutching her stomach. "Oh, I am never forgetting this because this is gold."

Rowan smiles, slow and knowing, his gaze never leaving Poppy's. "I'm very particular about my ride."

Poppy sputters at Rowan's implications. "I… we… Clara, stop laughing!"

Amber grins, finally letting go of the tire and clambering out of it. "Well, as long as someone's getting some traction." She walks over and offers her hand. "Nice to meet you, Rowan. Poppy has told me all about you!"

"I have not!" Poppy exclaims.

Clara giggles. "True, she has been pretty vague about you, but it's enough to make us curious. What are your intentions with our friend over here?"

Rowan glances between the pair of them, recognizing both of her friends' protective sides, stepping in now that the humor had diminished. "Well, I have no specific intentions and so I am playing it by ear. We have our first date at the Harvest Moon Festival."

Clara spins to scowl at Poppy. "Wait, we were supposed to go on a hayride together that night. You promised!"

"And she will. She already informed me that she had made those plans. I am taking her to dinner beforehand."

"Ok good. Just remember, she is mine before she is yours!"

"I will."

Amber moves up and drapes an arm over Clara's shoulder. "And she's mine after Clara!"

"So third in line." Clara replies.

Rowan arches a brow. "As expected I suppose. What's the saying? Hens before men."

Amber waggles her finger at him. "For a farmer like you, perhaps. In the city, it's chicks before dicks."

Poppy steps up beside them. "And here I thought it was dolls before balls. That's what Grams always said."

Rowan chuckles, his eyes darkening as they turn Poppy's way. "I can see your Grams saying that. She was a spitfire every time I dealt with her."

"That she was..." Her eyes connected with his, drawn to the depths of his eyes and feeling her body warm beneath his gaze.

Moments later, Clara nudges her. "Earth to Poppy."

Poppy drags her eyes from him and turns to Clara, mumbling distractedly. "What?"

Amber snickers. "Clara wants to know if that look means we should give you two some privacy."

"That is not..."

Amber glances between Rowan and Poppy. "Oh, it certainly is. I wonder if I should be taking notes for my future romance, because damn, that was intense. I think I want a farm boy now."

Rowan drags his eyes from Poppy, looking over the three of them. "I should go. It was a pleasure to meet you Amber. Clara, I will see you around town. Poppy… I will see you on Tuesday?"

"Yes. Tuesday." Poppy mumbles.

Rowan turns around and pulls himself effortlessly up on Ebonwind. He gives a nod to each of them and guides his horse back the way he came.

The three of them watch him fade in the distance before Amber and Clara turn on Poppy.

"Damn gurl! You have it bad."

"I do not!"

Amber drags Poppy over to the picnic blanket and sits down. "Yes, you do! I was beginning to wonder if Rowan dragged you into some smoldering romance novel in your head."

"Amber! That's not the case. It's just his eyes are amazing, and sometimes, I forget to look away."

Clara snickers, glancing at Amber. "Just how deep do those eyes go, because you were clearly drowning in them."

Poppy slaps her hands over her face. "You two! I should never have brought you together, let alone out here, to meet Rowan."

Clara nudges her. "Hey, to be fair, I already knew Rowan. If I wasn't in the man-hating era of my life, then I would be all over that."

Amber laughs. "Well, I don't think you have the chance now. He's all about his Poppy high. That much is clear." Turning to Poppy, she slaps her leg playfully. "You need to tap that boy and get it out of your system before you return."

Clara snaps her gaze over to Poppy. "Wait, return?"

Poppy sighs. "Yes, I am only here for six weeks Clara, remember? Then I have to return to the fashion world, especially if I want to make my name known around the world."

"Damn, and here I thought you had fallen in love and were sticking around."

"Unfortunately, no. Amber covered my debut launch, but there is still a lot that needs to happen."

"Well, if you ever need a break, I have a spare room."

Poppy laughs. "Sounds good."

The three of them lounge on the picnic blanket, enjoying leftover pizza and small talk, before heading back to the house to continue their sleepover inside. Monday afternoon they pack up, each saying their goodbyes with Amber promising to try to return for the harvest weekend festival. Poppy watches them both drive away and pads into the living room, collapsing on the beds she has yet to put away. Her thoughts drift from the fantastic weekend with her friends, over to Rowan and wondering what a sleepover with him would entail, knowing it would be unlike anything with the girls.

Spiced and Enticed

Two weeks pass in a steady rhythm. With the corn harvested, Poppy spends more days at the market, working to sell off the remaining crops and pottery. Afterward, she does her shopping. Even daring to step into the Cloth Depot, wandering the aisles and running her fingers over fabrics, indulging in a few purchases. Her trips to the hardware store become less frequent now that the house repairs are nearly complete. On the days Clara doesn't drop by the market to keep her company, Poppy heads to the lumberyard instead, sharing lunch with her friend amidst the scent of fresh-cut wood. She makes sure she either pops into the lawyers office to check in and replenish her slush fund before heading home or call them after breakfast if she stays home.

When Rowan arrives, she helps him in the fields, harvesting the last of the crops, the bond between them growing emotionally in leaps and bounds, but neither of them step past the marker of friendship. In the evenings, she relaxes on the back porch with Pinecone and the chickens, refusing to acknowledge the cock that wakes her up every morning. Throughout this time, the remaining farmers collect their hay orders, either taking it all with a truck and trailer, or setting up a storage plan. Feeling eternally grateful and relieved when the list is done.

Saturday morning, after breakfast and making her daily call, Poppy sits outside, her eyes watching the chickens waddle around, knowing she only has one more week left. She smiles, looking forward to her first official date with Rowan at the Harvest Festival. A man who has been haunting her dreams and creating warm flushes throughout her body whenever she thinks of him or becomes lost in his green eyes. He is someone that calls to her in so many ways and makes her doubt her decision to return to the city. Her eyes lift to the bare fields, recalling the day she arrived with the hay swaying in the breeze and the house looking run down and weather worn. Not any longer. Everything looked great, and she had done it… well, with the help of Rowan, but still an accomplishment she never would have thought possible for her.

She rises from the porch and heads inside, deciding this morning she is going to play with the fabric she purchased from the Cloth Depot. Heading into the kitchen, she rifles through the drawers and pulls out a pair of shears. Testing the blade's edge, she mutters softly, cursing herself for not buying proper ones when she bought the fabric. Grabbing a soda, she heads back up to her room, losing herself in her designs.

Hours later, she glances at the clock, knowing she should start getting ready, especially if she wants to soak the pain from her shoulders. She had forgotten what working on the floor did to her, what with having an actual cutting table in her apartment. Gathering up her design, she places it back on her desk, happy with the progress. Heading straight into Grams' ensuite, she undresses and steps into the tub as the water runs in, adjusting the temperature hotter as her skin adjusts. A soft groan escapes her as the heat soothes the aches from her muscles, staying in it only as long as she dares and leaving just enough time to get ready still.

Stepping out, she dries herself off and pads back to her bedroom. Poppy sorts through her closet, trying on several outfits, before finally deciding on a pale green sundress with cream panels inset in the skirt. Pairing it with yoga shorts since she knows she'll be doing at least two hayrides tonight and hay can get rather prickly on bare skin.

Grabbing her untouched make-up bag, she carries it to the main bathroom and sets it on the counter. She rifles through it and pulls out some of her favorites, opting for a more natural look, rather than a city glam one. She adds a thin brown line along her lids and accents her lashes with deep black mascara. Pulling out a light tan gloss, she gently runs it over her lips, savoring the vanilla flavor that always accompanies it. Running her fingers through her hair, she tries to tame it, knowing it desperately needs a trim and opts to fluff up the edges to frame her face.

She lifts her gaze, smiling at the sound of the truck's tires crunching on the gravel. Grabbing a small purse, she stuffs her ID and keys into it and bounds down the stairs, slipping on a pair of white strappy sandals. Poppy opens the door, her eyes following the truck as it parks out front, a smile spreading across her face as Rowan steps out and approaches. She laughs when she sees he's wearing black jeans and a dark green button-down shirt. "Looks like we were on the same wavelength."

He chuckles. "Indeed. It's a green day, apparently. You look beautiful."

"Thank you." Poppy feels her cheeks warm with a blush at the compliment. "I suppose, though you would think with the harvest festival, we should have chosen reds and golds."

"Probably, but I don't own any. I prefer blues and greens."

"I noticed."

Rowan arches a brow. "So, does that mean you deliberately dressed to match me?"

"No, if that was the case, I would have picked the blue sundress with green accents. That way I would have guaranteed a match, but I thought that might be a bit much for our first date."

"I see."

Poppy laughs. "It's a girl thing. Besides, if I had a sundress in autumn colors upstairs, you would see me wearing it instead, but Grams chose the wardrobe and I haven't been shopping for clothes since I got here."

Rowan chuckles. "You can always do that after the market. There are clothing stores in town."

"I could, but Grams clearly knows my style. She did pretty damn good with everything she bought me. I don't need any more."

"Wait? Did I just hear that correctly? You, a fashion designer who creates clothing… Doesn't need any more?"

"Hey." She nudges his shoulder. "Just because I love designing clothes does not mean I need to have more than I can ever wear in a lifetime! Besides, if I buy all the clothes made by everyone else, how am I supposed to make money? Nope, the whole point of this is to have other people buy my designs, not me to buy theirs."

"True. Well, I hope you sell a lot." He offers her a hand. "Are you ready?"

Poppy smiles, clasping her hand in his. "I am. I am looking forward to it."

Rowan walks her over to the truck and helps her in, closing the door once she is settled. Bounding around to the driver's side, he slides in next to her and closes his door. After buckling up, he starts the engine and backs up, driving slowly down her long driveway towards town, noticing her staring out the window at the autumn trees. As they approach the outskirts of town, he glances her way with a half-smile. "You're awfully quiet. Getting cold feet about the festival?"

She scoffs, rolling her eyes. "Please. Just mentally preparing myself for an entire evening of pumpkin-flavored everything."

Rowan chuckles. "Careful, now. You're in Everdell. You badmouth pumpkins, and you might just find yourself run out of town, especially since half the farmers around here, plant them."

She laughs at his teasing. "I better watch it then." Her eyes drift outside the windows to the streets, already alive with people hanging strands of lights and lanterns, knowing as dusk falls, they will light up like fireflies dancing in the night sky. Kids run around with pumpkins hugged in their arms, placing them on benches and planters along their path, before turning and running back to the piles to grab another. Music drifts through the air, bringing a smile to her lips, recalling her time here with her Grams. "Wow, look how quickly they set everything up."

"It's a yearly thing, so they pretty much have it mastered now." Rowan parks the truck, hopping out to circle around and open her door, offering her a hand.

Poppy gives him a look, but accepts his offered hand, her fingers curling into his as she clambers out of the truck. "True. I remember Grams being here, and I was one of the pumpkin and gourd runners. *Place them wherever you can find a spot for them*, they said. Clara and I deliberately found the most obscure spot we could just to see if anyone would notice."

"Somehow, I can see the two of you doing that. In fact, I suspect if your other friend, Amber, had been raised here, she would be right there with you."

"She probably would. She was planning to come out this weekend, but something came up with her brother."

"Can I say I am not sad?"

"Excuse me?"

"Well, I already have to share you with Clara for a hayride. Is it wrong of me not to want to share you with Amber as well, especially on our first date?"

Poppy blushes. "You're right, but to be fair, I made plans with Clara before I met you. So really, it's you that's interrupting her date."

Rowan pulls her close, looking down into her eyes. "I suppose I owe her then."

Poppy nods, feeling heat flood her body at the closeness of him. Her lips part on their own accord as she looks up, recalling what his last kiss tasted like, and finds herself wanting another one.

Rowan caresses her cheek, leaning in and capturing her lips in a gentle kiss, tasting her sweetness as people bustled around them. He groans inwardly and pulls back. "Sorry, I meant to save that for later, but I couldn't resist."

Poppy's blush deepens. "You were planning to kiss me later?"

"Yes. Isn't that how all dates go? At the end of the night, when you drop the lady off at her home, you bestow a sweet goodnight kiss upon her lips."

Poppy laughs and pushes him away. "You have been reading too many poetry books."

"Perhaps or perhaps not. I suppose one day you will see my farmhouse and know what books I read."

"I suppose." Poppy's thoughts drift to his house, wondering what it would look like, and finding herself curious if it matched what she pegged him living in. It would definitely not be the light creams and greys that she painted her Grams' house in, that's for sure.

"Poppy?"

"Yes, sorry, my brain zones when it's thinking about things. Design things in particular."

"You were thinking about clothes? Am I not entertaining enough?"

She laughs, winking his way. "Oh, you are. It was your house that drew me away. I picture pastel blues and greens with cream colored curtains!"

Rowan chuckles at her teasing. "Far from it. Perhaps sometime this week, I will come get you on Ebonwind and bring you back for a visit."

"Deal."

Walking along beside him, hand in hand, she turns her attention back to the town, alive with the chatter of families talking to people behind stalls offering spiced cider, caramel apples, and fresh pies. The festival being everything small-town charm promises.

Wandering through the crowd, Rowan pauses at a cider stand. "Here, try one of these."

"What is it?"

"Pumpkin cider."

"That sounds…"

"Shhh." Rowan places fingers over her lips to stop her. He pulls out some cash and sets it on the counter, accepting the steaming cup from the vendor and handing it over to her. "Just try it before you knock it."

"Fine." She accepts the cup and takes a sip, sighing in delight. "Alright, that's actually pretty good."

"Told you. Don't knock the pumpkins."

She laughs, taking another sip as they wander through the stalls, stopping at a ring toss. "Oh, I want to try!" She hands her cup over to Rowan and steps up to the vendor. As she fishes in her purse for her money, Rowan slips a bill over. "Hey! I could have paid for it."

"It's my treat. I asked you on the date, after all."

"Yes, but you shouldn't pay for everything."

"Today I am. Tomorrow, you can pay."

Poppy giggles. "Assuming there is a tomorrow. Don't you have to win me over with this date?"

"I do." He lifts the cup and mildly shakes it. "How am I doing?"

"Only time will tell." Poppy teases, taking the rings from the man and steps over to the marker. Staring at the posts, she squints her eyes and tilts her head, calculating the distance between them. Looking over the rings, knowing there was only one post they were landing on because of the posts being too close together, which would force the ring over to the side. A smile crosses her lips as she tosses it towards the back right corner, watching the ring snag and spin around the post.

"Nicely done."

She tosses the second towards the same post, thinking she might have overshot it, but watches as it settles lightly around the post at the last minute. "Yes! Two for two!"

The vendor pipes up. "One more and you can choose a stuffed toy, young lady."

Poppy takes a deep breath, flicking the ring with precision, only for it to catch the post just before her target and settle at its base. "YES! I won!" Her eyes scan the rows of animals before she points decisively at the one on the end. "I know I'm going to regret this, but I want the rooster."

Rowan watches as the attendant unclips the plush bird and hands it over, a smirk crossing his lips. "And what are you naming the adorable little pecker?"

Poppy swats at him with the plushie, her lips twitching as she fights the smile. "Not Reginald, that's for sure."

"How about Fergus? Strong, dignified, and commands respect."

She snorts, giving him another playful whack. "Perhaps I will name him Rowan!"

Rowan leans in, voice dripping with amusement. "I suppose I should be flattered that you want to cuddle me at night."

Poppy hugs the stuffed rooster to her chest and caresses its head. "Oh, absolutely. I'll snuggle him close and tell him all my secrets, maybe even give him little kisses on the beak." A smile slips onto her lips as she looks up at him, mischief dancing in her eyes. "But don't worry, I won't let him get too cocky."

Laughter escapes Rowan at her antics, his eyes following the hand currently caressing the bird. He leans in and whispers. "Mmm. You sure you can handle that much of me in your bed? I'd hate for you to be overwhelmed."

She gasps dramatically, pressing a hand to her chest. "Oh, you're right. I'd wake up every morning to endless preening and puffed-up arrogance. Maybe I should name him Modesty instead."

Rowan shakes his head, grinning. "Nah, name him Lucky, since he's clearly getting more action than me."

Poppy chokes on a laugh, swatting him again with the stuffed rooster. "Oh, please! If I start whispering sweet nothings to a stuffed animal, feel free to stage an intervention."

Rowan leans in, lowering his voice. "Darling, if you ever start preferring a stuffed version of me over the real thing, I'll have no choice but to take matters into my own hands."

Poppy raises a brow, smirking. "Oh? And what exactly would you do?"

Rowan steps even closer, eyes dark with playful challenge. "Guess you'll just have to find out, won't you? Now, would you like me to carry your cock so that you can have your drink back?"

Poppy arches a brow, a light blush creeping across her cheeks at his closeness, resisting the urge to step closer. "Oh, how generous of you, offering to handle my cock for me. But I think I can manage both. Wouldn't want you getting too attached."

"Right, wouldn't want me brooding over it." He leans in just enough that she can feel the warmth of him. "Or worse…getting jealous, especially with the way you are caressing it currently."

Poppy clutches the stuffed rooster, her blush deepening. "Oh no, we can't have that! What if you start crowing at sunrise to compete?"

Rowan grins, voice low and teasing. "Poppy, if I were in your bed, I guarantee you wouldn't need an alarm clock."

Poppy nearly drops the stuffed rooster in shock. "Oh, for… You are impossible."

Rowan winks and steps back just enough to give her space. "And yet, you keep me around. Now, what do you say we go and have dinner before I lose you to Clara for the first hayride?"

"Why does she get the first?"

"Because I want the evening ride, after the sun sets, and the moon rises. The stars sparkling like diamonds in the night, matching the light I see within you. So I can hold you close and keep you warm as the air cools, having your scent wrap around me as I nuzzle your neck."

Realizing the mood shifted, Poppy opens her mouth to respond, only to snap it shut, uncertain how to take the blatant flirtation, if one can call it that. Feeling her cheeks burn with embarrassment, she looks down at her stuffie and mutters softly. "You have been reading too many of those poetry books again."

Rowan places a few fingers beneath her chin, lifting her gaze back to meet his. "It's not poetry. It's truth. I like you Poppy. I like you a lot and I hope I am not reading the signals wrong, that tells me you feel the same."

Poppy feels his heat warm her at his touch on her chin, gentle and yet commanding. One that calls to her inside and makes her start to rethink her life's plans. She sighs softly at his statements, having had none of her other boyfriends so open in their conversations, and resists the urge to remind him she's leaving in a week's time. Especially since every time she mentions it, he retreats from her, knowing that's a conversation for another day. One that may or may not include figuring out how to make a long distance relationship work. She finds herself nodding in agreement when she draws back to the present. "You are not wrong. I've just never had anyone court me like you are. It's unusual."

Rowan's brows furrow. "You have never been courted?"

"I have, just not like you. They brought me flowers, or chocolates. I mean, it's easy to stop at a store to buy things that have no meaning. You, on the other hand, offer yourself, by helping me harvest my fields, just because, and talking with me about everything." She gestures to the people bustling past them, laughter filling the air. "By bringing me to a festival and going on a hayride. Dates in the city are quiet dinners of light conversations or movies with no talking. Even the few relationships

I have had have been nothing compared to what I have shared with you these past five weeks, and we were not even officially dating."

Rowan chuckles, caressing her face lightly. "Perhaps not dating in your eyes, but I knew, the second I saw you in the market, that you were mine."

A slow smile spreads on Poppy's lips at his words. "Possessive much?"

Rowan steps close, lowering down to whisper in her ear. "Yes, when I decide what's mine, I go for it, and you, my dear Poppy, are mine."

"POPPY! ROWAN!"

Poppy blushes and stumbles back, fanning herself with her rooster as she scans the crowds, recognizing Clara's voice anywhere, suddenly feeling grateful for her appearance. "Clara!"

Clara bounds up to them, her eyes darting between the two of them. "I didn't interrupt, did I?"

"No, it's fine. What are you doing here?"

"It's the festival Silly! Since you were so caught up in Rowan over here, I wanted to remind you that you owe me a hayride!"

Rowan smiles. "She knows. You get her after we have had dinner."

"Perfect. What time will that be?"

Rowan tilts his wrist, mentally calculating the time it was now and the time he wanted for dinner. "An hour and a half."

"Great!" Clara drags Poppy in for a hug, whispering in her ear. "No standing me up girl cause I want to hear all about the heat I saw coming off the pair of you moments ago." With that, she gives a nod to Rowan and races off into the crowd.

Poppy blushes, her eyes following her friend as she disappears. "Right. Can we say awkward?"

Rowan laughs and pulls her in close, draping an arm over her shoulder possessively. "Not at all. Let's go get dinner, shall we? Where we can talk about the weather and what the sports teams are doing."

Poppy shakes her head, a smirk crossing her lips at his taunts. "You are so bad. Perhaps I should abandon you before dinner."

"Not a chance, Poppy. I have you now. I will only give you up for one hayride, and that's only because Clara scares me just a little."

Bursting into laughter, she snaps her gaze up to his. "She does not!"

"You're right. She doesn't. But it lightened the mood."

She nudges him with her shoulder. "Yes, it did."

Rowan leads her further down the street as the smell of food wafts in the air. He guides her around a few of the booths and down a narrow passage between tents, stopping at a solo table tucked in the corner. "Madam, your table awaits."

"How did you know this was here?"

He chuckles and kisses her cheek. "I arranged it. Food is on its way."

"When?"

"Before I picked you up. Now, I did take the liberty of ordering for you, but if you don't like it, we can always slip out to the booths and get something else." Rowan pulls out the plastic chair and holds it for her.

"Fancy!" Poppy slides into the chair and helps to adjust herself to face the table. She places her plushie on the table beside her. "Now you have me curious."

Rowan smiles, and settles in across from her. He taps the tent beside him, feeling the answering tap from the other side. "It's on its way."

She laughs. "I should run around and see what food booth that is?"

"I would tackle you before you got too far. Wouldn't want to ruin my surprise."

"Somehow, I can see you doing that."

A few minutes later, a man walks around carrying a tray, setting it down on the table between them. "Bon Appetit!"

Poppy looks at the tray, her eyes snapping up to Rowans. "Sushi? You got me sushi? How?"

Rowan grasps his chest dramatically, his eyes dancing in devilish delight. "I'm hurt. Sometimes I do actually pay attention."

Poppy scowls at him, despite the laughter in her voice. "That's not what I meant."

"I know."

"So, how did you get sushi out here in booniesville?"

"I called Clara, who called Amber, who told me what restaurant you liked. Knowing one of the food vendors was coming from the city, I had them pick it up. So I will admit, it's not as fresh as I would like it, but from what I hear, as long as it's kept cold, it's fine."

Poppy's eyes light up as she pulls a plate of rolls towards her. "It's fantastic. The only one that's not good cold is unagi. That's gotta be warm, but these are great. You picked well."

"Amber picked. Not me. Now, please tell me what I am eating."

She laughs, pointing at the roll. "This is rice, as you know. The dark green paper looking wrap is called nori. It's a dried seaweed delicacy. There are other types, but nori is the most commonly used. Inside each roll varies. There is cucumber, salmon, avocado and cream cheese in this one. It's not traditional, but it's amazing. Some places deep fry it, which makes it even better. The other I like is crab instead of salmon. You can also get nigiri where they lay a small slab of raw fish, like salmon, tuna, tako, or rather octopus on rice, but it would not travel as well, I think."

Rowan grimaces at the thought. "Raw fish? Good thing I didn't get any of that nigiri, then."

Chuckling, she points to the roll in front of him. "It is, except sometimes that one has raw salmon in it too."

"Right… When I said I can get you different food if you didn't like it, I should have included myself in that statement." He suspiciously pokes at the rolls in front of him.

"You're just lucky the restaurant we like prefers the smoked variety." Poppy smiles and pops a roll in her mouth, rolling her eyes in delight as she savors the taste.

Rowan breathes a sigh of relief and tastes the first one, enjoying the unique flavors in his mouth. After swallowing, he nods. "It's not bad. Not what I expected."

"It's definitely an acquired taste. I know it's faux pas to talk about ex's on dates, but an ex introduced me to it. I was much more resistant than you were the first time."

Rowan smiles. "Hey, ex's make us who we are. They are a part of the past and sometimes inescapable when it comes to talking about where we came from."

"True."

"As long as you don't start comparing us."

Poppy giggles. "Pretty sure none of my ex's compare to you."

"What? Only pretty sure?"

A gleam enters Poppy's eyes as she meets his gaze. "Well, there are some things that I can't make a basis of comparison on… Yet."

Rowan's eyes darken, desire simmering in their depths as his gaze drifts from her eyes to her lips, then lower still. "Is that so? Perhaps we should do something about that later."

Poppy shifts in her chair, heat pooling in her core at the way he looks at her. If he were to throw her over his shoulder and carry her home right now, she knows damn well she wouldn't stop him. Instead, she meets his gaze with a slow smirk, wondering why he instilled so much bravery within her. "I'll be counting the minutes."

His gaze snaps up to hers, immediately noticing the way her breath stills and her lips part, begging to be kissed. His jaw ticks as he resists every urge inside himself not to drive her home right now. "If only you had not promised a hayride to Clara, I might have been convinced to skip the rest of the festival."

Poppy tilts her head, feigning deep consideration as she taps a finger against her chin. "Well, technically, she asked me first, and I have known her longer."

"Indeed. I might have a few very compelling arguments about why you should ditch her and let me take you home, but for now, I'll play the gentleman."

Poppy lets out an exaggerated sigh, her eyes dancing in humor. "Shame. I do love a man who takes initiative."

"Careful. Keep teasing me like that, and all promises are off the table."

Poppy bursts out laughing. "Alright. I will behave. I mean, I have this amazing sushi to eat that my date imported, especially for me, and I wouldn't want it to go to waste."

Rowan winks. "That's right. Besides, I have enough patience to wait a few more hours."

"That's good." She pops another piece of sushi in her mouth, enjoying the delightful taste.

An hour later, they gather the stuffed rooster and the empty containers, sorting them into trash and recycling before heading toward the hayrides. Laughter fills the air as kids race past, forcing them to weave around the chaos. The chatter of festival-goers blends with the soft music drifting from speakers perched atop the vendor stalls. Fifteen minutes later, they near the barns, where horses shift impatiently, eager to be off, their ears flicking as people clamber into the wagons hitched behind them.

Poppy scans the waiting crowd, searching for Clara. She spots her off to the side, chatting with a few familiar faces from the market. Grinning, she lifts a hand and waves. "Clara!"

Clara spins, says a quick goodbye to her group, and jogs over. "Pops! You made it! I was starting to think Rowan had whisked you away."

Poppy hands her stuffed rooster over to Rowan and hugs Clara before stepping back with a grin. "Oh, he tried, but I told him you had dibs."

"Damn right, I do. Now, come on!" Clara grabs her hand and drags her toward the wagons.

Laughing, Poppy glances back at Rowan. "I'll see you when we get back!"

"I'll be waiting." His gaze lingers on her, enjoying the enthusiasm the two of them have when they are together.

Clara, already climbing onto the wagon, wags a finger at him. "Mine, remember."

"For one hayride." Poppy teases, laughing as they settle into the hay.

The wagon lurches forward as the driver clicks the horses into motion. Once they're past the glow of the festival lights, Clara rolls onto her side, propping herself up on one elbow. "Alright. Spill."

Poppy exhales, her lips curving into a soft smile as her thoughts drift to Rowan. "Spill what?"

Clara nudges her. "You know what I want to hear."

Poppy groans, flopping onto her back. "Ugh, fine. No, it hasn't happened yet. But tonight? If I didn't have plans with you, we'd already be halfway home."

Clara lets out an excited squeal. "Poppy! I knew it! I'm so happy for you! You guys are perfect together."

"Yes, well, there is the catch. I am leaving in a week and we don't talk about it because Rowan gets moody and withdraws whenever I mention it."

"Can you not stay?"

"Not really. Fashion is a city life. If I want my designs to succeed, I have to be there; promoting, networking, making sure the right people see them." Poppy sighs in dismay and closes her eyes for a moment. "The industry moves fast. It's all about nightlife, parties, events. Designers dress people in their creations and take them to those parties, hoping to catch the eye of someone famous. Three of my designs made the Up-and-Coming list at the World Fashion Day show. If I stay here, I can't do any of that… and it's what I went to school for."

"I get that. How about a long distance thing? You come home on your weekends, which would be what, Monday and Tuesdays?"

"Yes. Gatherings are Thursdays through Sundays, for the most part. It's doable I suppose, but the time spent driving, and being here, would be designing time. Plus, it's a farm. It's going to require more time than I can give it. I suppose if I got together with Rowan, we would be living together, so there is that. I don't know. It's complicated. I feel like I am being torn in two."

Clara reaches over and draws Poppy into her arms. "I am sure you will figure it out. Tonight we have a hayride to enjoy and then you have Rowan to enjoy!"

Poppy laughs and snuggles into her friend. "I do. Thanks Clara, for being my friend."

"Always! We are besties! You are stuck with me."

Twenty minutes later, the driver guides the wagon into the back of the line and stops. Poppy and Clara clamber off, giving each other a hug goodbye.

Spotting Rowan standing off to the side, rooster in hand, Clara pushes Poppy in his direction. "Have fun!"

Poppy chuckles and heads in his direction, her eyes roaming over his casual stance, before locking on his eyes. "Rowan."

"Did you have fun?"

"I did."

"Did you want another one?"

"I… No."

Rowan takes her and pulls her close. "Then I can take you home?"

"You can."

"Perfect." He drapes an arm over her shoulder, steering her back toward the truck. After helping her in, he places the rooster in her lap and shuts the door, striding around to the driver's side and starts the engine. Carefully weaving through the throngs of festival goers, he drives out of town, the road quieting as they head toward Poppy's place. But instead of stopping out front, he pulls up beside the barn and parks.

Poppy arches a brow, a light teasing entering her voice. "Barn maintenance at this hour?"

"Not quite." Rowan hops out, and swings open her door, offering a hand to help her down. Then, heading to the back of the truck, he returns with a small, old-fashioned radio and a blanket draped over his arm. With a flick of a switch, soft music crackles to life, floating into the night air.

Poppy stares at him. "You're serious?"

He extends a hand, eyes glinting. "Come on, city girl. One dance won't kill you."

She hesitates for only a second before slipping her hand into his. "Alright."

Rowan leads her inside the barn, where the aromatic scent of hay wraps around them. Placing the radio on the bench, he spreads the blanket over a low pile of hay. Turning around, he pulls her close, one hand circling her waist, the other clasping hers under the soft glow of the moonlight. They sway in slow circles; the music filling the quiet spaces between them.

Poppy feels her pulse skip, the warmth of Rowan's touch grounding her in a way that sends shivers up her spine. "You're quite a good dancer," she murmurs, tilting her head up to look at him.

He grins. "You sound surprised."

"I am. Being a farm boy, I half expected line dancing or something." Poppy laughs softly, resting her head against his chest. The steady thrum of his heartbeat, the strength of his arms around her, and the subtle warmth of his scent make the rest of the world fade away. For the first time in a long time, she wonders if, just maybe, home is in Everdell.

Rowan rests his chin atop her head, holding her close as she melts into him. Releasing her hand, he wraps both arms around her, savoring the quiet perfection of the moment. A few songs later, he pulls back, tilting her face up with gentle fingers. Their eyes meet for the briefest of heartbeats before he leans in, capturing her lips with his. The kiss deepens as she succumbs to him, sending a wave of desire flooding through him. Breaking the kiss moments later, he scoops her up and places her on the blanket, crawling in beside her. "Poppy, I know we joked about this, but I don't want to overstep…"

She presses her fingers to his lips, silencing him with a knowing smile. "Shhh, Rowan. Tonight, I'm yours. Tomorrow, we'll figure everything else out."

His eyes darken, filled with something deeper than just desire. "You are truly amazing." He traces the curve of her jaw, his touch featherlight, before capturing her lips again, this time, intending to lose himself in her.

Both of them are oblivious to the fact that the air cools around them as the moon dips lower in the sky, each exploring, tasting and learning the other in ways only lovers can.

Oaths and Echoes

September 21

Monday morning, Poppy groans in dismay, her hand reaching out to the empty bed beside her, surprised at how quickly she adapted to having Rowan here for the weekend. She pulls a pillow over her head and rolls over, trying to drown out the rooster demanding his food. Pushing herself out of bed, she spots the note on her nightstand. Picking it up, she smiles at his flowing script.

Sorry, you looked so peaceful sleeping. I just couldn't wake you to say goodbye. Animals and the farm needed tending. I will be back this afternoon. Yours always, Rowan.

Sighing softly, she picks up the pillow next to her and presses her face into it, breathing in his scent. Placing it in her lap, she glances at the rumpled blankets, smiling at how well she slept tangled in his arms, drawing laughter from her. "Hah Grams. Two of us CAN fit in my bed." Knowing she should get on with it, she places the pillow on her side of the bed and heads down to the kitchen, spotting the coffee already made. "Damn, I could get used to this."

An hour later, Poppy sits at the computer, searching through the local realtors for one that appeals to her. Knowing they will come out and let her know what still needs fixing now that it is closing in on the six weeks of her term here. She flips through absently, reading their qualifications before stopping on one, liking the looks of her profile.

Picking up her cell, she scowls at the lack of service. Some things never change. Jotting the number down, she walks down the hallway to the landline, dialing the agent's number. As it rings, it sounds in time with the rooster suddenly crowing outside, making her wonder what ruffled his feathers this late in the morning. Her eyes stray to the window, watching Pinecone jump up on the ledge and sidle her way in. Smiling, she turns her attention to the woman that answered.

"Good morning, Everdell Reality. Sharon speaking."

"Hi. My name is Poppy. I am looking to sell the property that I am inheriting from my Grams, so I was wondering if you could come out and see what needs to be done to make it marketable."

"Sure, let me check my calendar. When were you thinking?"

"Any morning this week is fine." Poppy shifts away from Pinecone, weaving between her legs and meowing loudly, blending with Big Red outside who had increased his tempo, making it difficult for Poppy to hear anything on the phone. She covers the phone with her hand, muttering at the cat. "Shhh Pinecone. You and that bloody rooster need to shut up. I am trying to talk."

"Sounds like you have your hands full there with a houseful of animals?"

"No, just two. A barn cat…Hey! Ouch, that's my leg. And Sir Peck's-a-lot outside that I am going to broil soon." Poppy rubs her calf where the cat's claws just dug into her, feeling the blood drip down her leg. "No. BAD cat! Sorry, it just clawed me. It hasn't done that before… HEY. NO! Look. Can I call you back? I gotta lock the cat outside and shut the cock up."

"Sure."

"Thanks." Poppy slams the phone down. "What the hell had gotten into you two?!" She goes to grab Pinecone by the scruff only to have her bolt up the stairs. "No, if you are going to be a miserable cat, you are not welcome inside." Poppy spots her darting through the open door into her Grams' room, and follows her in. Her eyes scan the room, seeing her dash beneath the bed. "Oh, you think so." Poppy gets down on her hands and knees and peers beneath it, seeing the cat tucked behind a decorative box. Sighing, she pulls the box out of the way, her eyes falling on the label.

Journals

Forgetting about the cat, she lifts the lid, seeing a variety of leather-bound books inside. Pulling one out, she flips through it and reads the perfectly written cursive. "Grams, I didn't know you kept journals." Tucking the journal back, she lifts the box and carries it back to her room, placing it on the end of her bed. Running downstairs, she grabs a soda and a water, and brings them back upstairs. She props her pillows up and curls against them, pulling the first journal out to read, starting when Grams was a teenager and had met her future husband, Callum Levens. Smiling at her first date, through to their marriage. Going through his desire for children with the failed attempts over the years.

Poppy swipes at the tears sliding down her face, her heart breaking for her Grams at the emotions she expressed in her words at being unable to have a child, suddenly dreading getting to the one where the car accident killed her daughter. Placing the journal down, she rises and runs to the bathroom, grabbing the box of tissues. Carrying it back, her eyes land on Pinecone, sleeping peacefully on her bed. "I should kick you outside, you stupid cat."

Poppy settles back in her corner of pillows and places the box beside her. Reaching out, she pets Pinecone for a few moments, smiling at the soft rumble coming from her chest before she picks up the next journal and flips it open. Her eyes scan the pages, smiling when Gram mentions meeting Kaelen, remembering him from her childhood, always helping around the farm. How the farm prospered under his touch and with it came the excitement of finally becoming pregnant. How ecstatic Gramps was, and how he doted on her, not letting her do any of the farm work she was accustomed to doing. Even laughing at the grumpy comments inserted about the overprotectiveness and stubbornness of her husband and how she is pregnant, not porcelain.

Poppy flips the page and stops, staring at an aged piece of parchment folded into the journal. Pulling it out, she flips it over in her hands, knowing instinctively that this was far older than even the journals she is reading. Her fingers caress the fragile paper, not the normal standard white, but one with an ancient feel to it. Unfolding it, she stares at the scripture surrounded by images in each corner, one she recognizes from her weekend with Rowan.

Her fingers trace the harvest moon, surrounded by falling leaves on the bottom left. Shifting over, she notes bare trees on the right, with what looks like swirling snow. In the upper right are stalks of wheat with a burning sun and on the left are budding flowers with rain droplets. Her gaze narrows, clearly recognizing the four seasons, but that doesn't explain why Rowan has one of them tattooed on his back. Turning her attention to the words, she reads through them slowly, feeling a well of panic growing as her stomach twists inside.

By root and river, by stone and sky, let it be known. This land and those who tend it are bound as one.

I, Rowan Wynthorn, Fae Guardian of Everdell, do enter into a sacred covenant with Rose Levens, bound by blood to the Line of Levens, sworn keepers of this land until such time that her Granddaughter Poppy McInnes can step into her place due to the loss of her daughter. In exchange for Everdell's continued bounty; its fertile fields, flowing waters, and abundant harvest, I offer my watchful eye, my guiding hand, and my sworn protection. So long as this pact is honored, the land shall flourish, and those who call it home shall know prosperity.

Respect the land as you would a life.

Take not in greed, nor leave it barren.

What is taken must be given back in kind.

Honor the old ways, including the festivals, the offerings and the rites of gratitude.

But heed this warning well:

The Levens line must hold Everdell, for it is their stewardship that anchors the pact, thus the land shall not be severed from its keeper. Should Everdell be sold, abandoned, or misused, is to unbind the pact and the spell that sustains it. The soil shall wither, the rivers shall turn to dust, and ruin shall fall upon this town. My protection shall fade, and the wild things beyond my reach shall reclaim what was lost.

Sealed by the will of the earth, by the breath of the wind, by the whisper of the river's song, and by the fire that warms Everdell's heart.

Signed in the season of first bloom, beneath the light of the Moon.

Rowan Wynthorn, Guardian of Everdell

Rose Levens, Keeper of the Lineage

Poppy stares at the parchment, her hands shaking as she tries to comprehend what this means. Clearly her Grams signed something that bound her to this land. Something that was supposed to bind her daughter and her granddaughter. Is this why Grams forced her to stay, so she wouldn't sell it and destroy her hometown?

She slaps the contract down and jumps out of the bed, her thoughts spinning a mile a minute as she stares at it in dismay. Wishing it would disappear, or that she would wake up to this being a dream. She shakes her head and backs up, slamming into a wall and sinking to the floor, tucking her knees in. It can't be real? Fae are not real. Rowan is not a fae. There is no way. He is very much a human. She's seen him naked. Fae have wings and there were definitely NO wings. She is pretty certain she'd remember that.

Closing her eyes, she drops her head to her knees. Fae, faeries, they are stories of myth and legend. But what if it is real? It looks authentic enough. But if he is, then that means he lied to her. Granted, she never actually asked him… who would? Are you a faerie? Anyone in their right mind would have her committed. But she did notice the crops and asked him about that. Country magic, my ass. It was his magic. Why didn't Grams tell her?! Why keep this secret when she was going to find out anyhow?

Pushing herself up, she pads to the bed and picks up the parchment, re-reading it, knowing deep within her heart that it was very much real. A heart that is now breaking. Seeing her dreams of being a fashion designer flying out the window, knowing that if she left to follow that dream, Everdell would die.

Anger flashes in her eyes, staring at the two names on the bottom. Rowan and her Grams had lied to her. Correct that. Both of them withheld information, but it was pretty damn important information as far as she is concerned. At least Grams had a reason. She probably planned to tell her, but then she died before she could. But Rowan, he is very much alive. He should have said something before he bedded her. Especially since he is clearly bound to Grams.

She paces back and forth at the edge of her bed. "What the hell, Grams?! You are forcing the decision out of my hands. You should have told me. Rowan is going to get an earful when I see him this afternoon 'cause I am pissed. When did he even sign this? Wait. How old is he?" Knowing contracts often have dates, she scans it again to no avail. Her eyes land on the journal she found it in, wondering if her Grams had written it in there.

She snatches it up and plops back down on the bed to read it, knowing she needed more ammunition when she confronted Rowan, since she can't confront her Grams. Better yet, when she called her lawyer today, she would ask him as well. He had to know because Grams re-adjusted the Will with him, and she saw Josh and Rowan talking at the market. Though if he was not in on this, then it would be doubtful her Grams would have said anything.

Flipping back to where she left off, Poppy settles in to read, discovering that the pact has bound her family to the land for generations. It was first forged by Rose's ancient ancestor, Marie Melantine, during a time of great need; when she pledged her lineage to the fae in exchange for the village's survival. Since then, the pact had passed down through the eldest heir of each generation, but only when the cycle of the guardian aligns with that of the keeper. Some inherited it at twenty, others at thirty, and some only upon the passing of the previous keeper. That both the keeper and the guardian are bound to uphold the land's prosperity, their roles tied to the contract until the next pair take their place.

Yet, as Poppy reads on, a question gnaws at her. If Rowan had been her grandmother's guardian, why hadn't he retired when she passed? Clara had mentioned he'd only been here a few years, but if the guardian is meant to serve alongside the keeper, shouldn't he have always been here?

She takes a few calming breaths as she reaches for her water. Something stronger would be preferable, but she needs a clear head to process this. Tomorrow, she can drink. Today, she needs answers. Reading on, she discovers Rowan is not, in fact, her grandmother's guardian. That role belongs to someone else; Kaelen Stormvale. Frowning, she picks up the parchment again, staring at Rowan's signature at the bottom. Her fingers trace the ink, and she mutters under her breath. "That's certainly not Kaelen Stormvale's name."

Before she can process her thoughts, a soft glow shimmers in the dimly lit room. The book slips from her hand as the air thickens with magic. The light grows brighter before dimming again. When it fades, Poppy's eyes land on a man she instantly recognizes, long golden hair, braided in three strands with green eyes eerily like Rowan's. One who stood alongside her Grams in helping around the farm and raising her after the accident killed her parents. Her voice wavers. "Uncle K-K?"

"Poppy."

"But...You... How?"

Kaelen chuckles and approaches the bed, sitting beside her. "Because you called me."

"No, I didn't."

"Yes, Poppy. My full name is Kaelen Stormvale. You spoke it aloud and because you are a keeper, it called me forth."

"What? No! I am just Poppy."

"You are by your bloodline, a Levens, and therefore a keeper."

"I am a McInnes!"

"Just because your mother married into another name, does not mean you are not a Levens, or rather, a Melantine. While the name on the contract changes, the bloodline does not. Just as your Grams and your mother before you, so will follow your son or daughter. Although your mother was never a keeper."

"According to her journal, you are Grams' guardian, but according to the contract, Rowan is. Why is that?" She picks it up and stuffs it in his hands. "And what the hell is going on?"

Kaelen holds the parchment, reading the script he is familiar with. "It's complicated, but I will do what I can to explain it. Guardians arrive several years before the passing of the old, before the keeper is notified of what's going to happen. This way they may get to know their keeper and integrate themselves into their lives to make the bonding easier."

Poppy rubs her temples. "This is so unreal and confusing. I have so many questions."

"I am sure you do, and I will answer them as you ask."

"How are you so young? I watched you age?"

"We age as you do in the mortal realm, but when we return home, we regain our youthful appearance."

"So you were always around Grams then."

"Yes."

"So what happened to Grams? She was strong for her age. They couldn't even determine the cause of death."

"That's our fault. The maximum term a keeper is to maintain is fifty years. After that, the faerie magic starts to unbind, and it's a drain on a keeper's soul. With the passing of your mother, the contract never transferred, and you were too young to take it over. Normally it's in your twenties or thirties, depending on when the last generation received it. Your Grams knew the contract should have passed to you as soon as you turned sixteen because of the missed generation, but she wanted you to have the freedom of choice. One that allowed you to finish high school and follow your desires into design school. So she kept her name on the paper longer than she should have, knowing it would cost her to grant you your happiness."

"Maybe she didn't know?" Poppy closes her eyes, feeling tears spring back into them, knowing once again, Grams put her wants and desires first.

"She knew Poppy. Rowan arrived in town to transfer the contract over to save her, but you were already gone. Your Grams refused to let us interfere with your schooling, but we are fae and Daine had already followed you. He was watching over you because it is a protected line. We already lost your mother. We were not losing you too."

"Wait, who is Daine?"

"Your mother's guardian, but he arrived too late."

"Too late for what?"

"To save your mother." Kaelen sighs, his eyes shifting over to the dresser with Rose's picture on it. "To back up a bit, each guardian is tied to the seasons, as are you. With us, it shows as a tattoo on our back that shifts with the seasons… These images here, they are the marks of the season and tied to what's displayed on our backs. In the autumn, falling leaves and a harvest moon. Winter is bare trees and swirling frost. Spring is budding flowers and rain droplets and summer is golden wheat and a burning sun. That is why you rarely see us remove our shirts, because how would we explain that to normal people?"

"I guess that would be hard. I have seen Rowan's tattoo just recently. It matches that one." She points to the corner with the falling leaves and harvest moon.

"I have one too, and so does every guardian that has ever stepped foot in your realm."

"I always wanted a moon tattoo."

"That's because you are a fall keeper. Your Grams was a spring keeper. Now, as I said, we usually arrive a few years before the bonding to get to know our keeper."

"I read about that in Gram's journal."

He nods. "Daine had just arrived, a few months before the crash, so there was no bonding between them yet. I don't even know if she had met him, to be honest. You see, each keeper only has one season tied to them, and we can only bond when the seasons match and the moon aligns them together. Your mother still had a year and a half before that was to happen, so the protection wasn't there, but he did bond with you when he pulled you from the wreck. Your Grams was quite clever. Since she lost our daughter, she bargained to have Daine watch you until you were old enough to get your own guardian."

"Wait, our?"

"Yes, our. Now, it is not unusual for a guardian to fall in love with the keeper and vice versa because there is a blood bond between them. One that cannot be broken. Your Grams... Rose, as I called her, was my link to this world, and she was happily married to her husband Callum, but there were complications in that relationship. She loved Callum with all her heart, but her heart was torn, because she loved me as well. It was late one night when I found her beneath the willows, crying. Her and Callum had fought because she could not give him the child he desperately wanted. And so I did. Through that love, she conceived your mother, Aisley. Callum didn't know, and it was a secret we never spoke of again... until now. He was overjoyed to find out, believing it to be his, but I could see the fey touch upon her."

"But what about you? You got shafted, watching another raise your daughter."

"Yes, and No. Yes, she was my biological daughter, but for all intents and purposes, she was Callum's pride and joy. He loved Aisley with everything he had and that made Rose happy, so I was happy. Besides, I wasn't entirely shafted because I worked on the farm and got to be Uncle K-K to you."

"That's kinda sad."

"It can be the life of a guardian. Rose and I agreed to keep it a secret, and so we did. This is where things get complicated. Rose kept the guardian-keeper contract from your mother, and judging by your reaction, she didn't tell you either. Probably because your mother fell in love with your father Malcolm and Rose wanted her to have a normal life. One without worrying about another man in the picture that would call to her, pulling her in two directions like she had to deal with. One to her husband and one to Daine, especially when she got pregnant with Malcolm's child. The downside to that, is it left her without a guardian to protect her. The unseelie..."

"Wait, what is the unseelie?"

"Some would call them evil. We call them the dark court. The guardians come from the light court."

"I see..."

"Well, you don't yet, but hopefully you will by the end of this conversation. The unseelie are the ones that cause plants to wither, the rivers to run dry, and all manner of chaos tied to that. It's what they feed on. When your ancestor Marie approached us, she drew their attention, which is why we agreed to the pact. Because your parents didn't have full protection yet, the unseelie used their powers and caused the accident. While not bonded, Aisley still had a guardian. He sensed her distress but arrived too late. He could only pull you from the car before it burst into flames, killing everyone in it."

"So it wasn't an accident?"

"No, it was deliberate. Daine stayed nearby until the police arrived and took you away."

"I don't remember anyone pulling me out of the car."

"You were six. The trauma of the accident probably blocked your memories. After that day, Daine should have returned to the faerie realm, but he pledged to help your Grams with watching over you. Especially since she lost three of her family in that car crash."

"So I have seen this Daine then?"

"Yes. You called him Danial."

"The cute farm hand?"

"That would be the one."

Poppy slaps her hands to her face, as a deep blush crosses her cheeks. "Oh, my gawd! I had the biggest crush on him."

"I know, and so did he."

"That's even worse!" She groans in dismay.

Kaelen reaches out and pulls her hands down from her face. "Poppy. It was a childhood crush. It's perfectly normal and we accept them. That's part of being a keeper, they are naturally drawn to guardians."

"But he was Moms!"

"Yes, and Rowan is yours."

"Still doesn't answer why his name is on the parchment with Grams."

Kaelen lifts the parchment from his lap and waves his hand over it, watching the writing shift. "See, here is Daine's name, right next to mine." He shifts his hand over it to where he appeared next to Rose. "Because there was no daughter for Daine, we added him to your Grams as well until it was time for her to pass it over to you. When Rowan stepped into this world, I knew and so brought him to your Grams. She refused at first, but realized her time was drawing near and eventually signed the contract with Rowan, so he could add you after the fact. You see, when our keeper dies, we effectively do as well, but we return to the realm of the fey."

"That's why she changed her Will. So I would be forced to meet Rowan here."

"Yes."

"Can you leave Everdell?"

"We can, but not for longer than a few weeks. So we can take trips and go on holidays, but after that, both the keeper and the guardian must return."

Poppy grows silent, mulling over her thoughts and all that had been spoken. Her hands twist in her lap as she looks up into Kaelen's eyes. "She knew she was dying because of me?"

"Not because of you, Poppy, because of her. Rose was... Very giving. She placed everyone before her, because that was who she was."

"Right...."

Kaelen sighs, reaching out to take her hand and clasp it in his. "Poppy. This is not your fault. It's not hers either. It's circumstance. We lost your mother too soon. That never should have happened, but your Grams, she wanted her family happy. She took a risk, hoping to survive long enough for you to finish your five years of schooling, and become a success, but unfortunately, it didn't pan out for her. I think she was hoping for another year or two, and then she could transfer you over to Rowan, but the fae drain is a genuine thing."

Tears spill from Poppy's eyes. "I wish she was still here. To have her arms around me and hold me, telling me it's okay and to follow my heart."

Kaelen wraps an arm around her and pulls her close. "Shhh. Your Grams loves you and is watching over you, even as we speak."

Poppy leans against him, resting her head on his chest. "How do you know?"

"I probably should not be telling you this, but everything about your generation has broken the rules already. What's not written in the contract is that when a keeper dies, they join us in the land of the fae. I have been helping your Grams adjust, so to speak."

Poppy snaps her head up to stare at him. "Can I talk to her?"

"Unfortunately, no. Not until it's your time to join us, and don't be killing yourself to do that."

"But I will see her again?"

"Yes."

"What about mom?"

"Yes... Only because she is my daughter, otherwise we would have lost her soul due to not being bonded."

"So when I am old and die, I'll be reunited with them again."

"Correct."

"I just need to do this thing with Rowan and not leave this town... Ever."

"Well, no, not ever. You can go away for weekends at a time, or take vacations, as I said. Just limited to two weeks."

"Wait, so you said Danial... Daine was watching over me. How is that possible? Especially since I don't remember my childhood crush being there."

Kaelen smiles and hands the parchment over to her. "Call him and find out."

"Call him?"

"You are a keeper. Speak his name. Normally, you would not have access to this, but again, your Grams broke a lot of rules. Hell, you can even summon Rowan here if you wanted."

Poppy glances between Kaelen and the parchment, disbelieving that she had the power. She murmurs the name softly. "Daine Cairos." Her eyes lift as the lights shimmer once more and Daine appears in the room before her. Seeing him, she narrows her eyes. "Wait, you were the janitor in my dorm!"

"I was. Now I am a part time tenant downstairs in your apartment due to the fact that I have to return here to recharge." Daine chuckles and turns to his friend. "Kaelen, first, what are you doing here, and second, why are you outing us?"

"Rose outed us actually by keeping journals and Poppy here called me forth. I have been trying to explain everything."

Daine smiles, offering a hand out to Poppy. "Nice to meet you as Daine Cairos, and not Danial or Cyrus."

Poppy accepts his hand, shaking her head at the same time. "I don't know how I didn't recognize you. Now that I see you here, I should have."

"Different location, and I glamoured myself."

"And aged."

"Yes, we do age as you do while in this realm."

"So Rowan will too?"

"He will."

"What if I meet someone else?"

Kaelen smiles. "You have met Rowan. There will be no others that can take your affections."

"But Grams had Gramps and Mom had Dad?"

"Yes, and they met them before their guardian. Did any at your school appeal to you?"

"No."

"Does Rowan?"

Poppy stops, her gaze bouncing from Kaelen to Daine, chewing on her lower lip as she resists answering what she knows is already in her heart. Sighing softly. "Yes, but I am still mad at him. He should have told me before we…." A blush crosses her cheeks at where her words nearly went.

"He probably should have, yes, but there might be a reason for it."

"Well, he has been kind of hot and cold towards me."

"Interesting. Why don't you call him and let's find out?"

"I can do that with him, too?"

"Yes."

"But I have said his name several times already, and he's not here."

Kaelen hovers his hand over the parchment, restoring it to the current contract. "Not his last name."

"Right. Rowan… Wait, it just calls you from where you are?"

"Yes."

"What time is it?" She leans around Kaelen to look at the clock, seeing it was well after lunch and he was due to arrive soon. "I think I will wait. He is probably driving here and I don't want to do that."

Daine chuckles. "Oh sure, pull me here, but not him."

Poppy scowls his way. "I didn't think about it at the time. There is quite a bit going on in my head. Were you doing anything important?"

"No, I actually followed you home. I have been hanging under the willows with Rook."

"Who's Rook?"

"The crow that's been following you around."

"I didn't notice."

"You weren't supposed to."

"Is he a fae too?"

"No, they are just animals we make a connection with to have a second or third set of eyes."

Her eyes glance over to Kaelen. "Do you have one?"

"Not since I left with your Grams, but Reginald was mine."

"Figures you would choose the cock. I guess that's why Grams has them all over the house."

"Well, she loved mine, if that's what you're getting at."

"Eww Uncle K-K!! I don't want to hear that! So what's Rowans?"

Kaelen and Daine glance at each other. "We don't know for certain, but if we were to hazard a guess, she's on your bed."

"Wait, Pinecone? The cat?"

"Yes, she's close and doesn't seem phased by two fae in the room. Normally animals react to our presence."

"Well, that explains a lot."

"What do you mean?"

"It's just that when I was on the phone to…" Poppy pauses, hearing the truck approaching the house, something she found she looked forward to daily now. "Rowans here." Rising, she runs from the room and down the stairs, stopping at the front door to watch him park. Feeling Kaelen and Daine approaching behind her, she glances up and shoos them off to the side. "He doesn't need to know you are here yet."

"He knows Poppy. We always know where the other fae are."

"Of course you would." She watches Rowan slide from the truck and close the door after him, noticing his eyes slipping behind her to her two guests. Despite the anger flaring inside at his keeping this secret from her, she forces a smile to her lips as he approaches. "Rowan."

"What's going on Poppy?"

"I think you have something to tell me."

Rowan narrows his eyes as he stops on the deck before them, his hands landing on his hips as his shoulders stiffen at the implications. "You were not ready to be told, and they should not have done it."

Kaelen places a hand on Poppy's shoulder to keep her silent. "We didn't. Rose did. Apparently, she left journals available for Poppy to read, with the contract tucked inside them. I only helped clarify some things."

"What are you doing here Kaelen? Shouldn't you be with Rose?"

"Poppy read my name while holding the contract."

"I see. And you Daine? You were to remain hidden until I convinced her."

"Summoned as well." Daine shrugs his shoulders.

Poppy scowls at Rowan. "This is not their fault. It's yours. You should have told me."

"And say what Poppy? That I am a fae and if you leave, Everdell dies? Or that I would wither away with it? No, you are already intent on selling this place. It would have driven you out of here faster."

Kaelen snaps his gaze to Poppy. "You're planning to sell?"

"She was on the phone with the realtor this morning, Kaelen." Rowan answers.

Poppy glares at him. "How do you know that?"

"Poppy, I am fae, and your guardian. Even when I am not here, I know what you are up to."

"Right, because you have the animals watching. No wonder Pinecone scratched the shit out of me when I was on the phone. And that bloody cock outside, crowing so loudly I couldn't even hear the lady on the other end."

Rowan shrugs his shoulders. "What can I say? I have a vested interest in you not selling."

"I see… And is that why Pinecone led me to Grams' journals?"

He frowns, his eyes darting to Kaelen. "No, I was unaware she was writing things down. I was not her guardian, despite the recent change in the contract. I was always yours, Poppy."

Poppy shakes her head, her hands going up to her temples, pressing her fingers into her skin to quell the pain. "I think I need to sit down." She spins and ducks past Kaelen and Daine, heading to the rocking chair in the living room. Plopping herself down, she closes her eyes and rocks, knowing by the footsteps, the others had followed her into the room. Rowan's scent surrounds her, and she cracks one eye, seeing him squatting before her. "What. This is very overwhelming."

"I understand."

"No, I don't think you do." She snaps back. "Faeries don't exist and yet, I have three of you in my living room saying you do. None of you even have wings. I mean, aren't faeries supposed to be able to fly? In all the books Grams read to me as a child, they were tiny and had wings! Then, all of you have signed a contract with my Grams, talking about being fae guardians of the land."

"Not of the land. We are guardians of you. You are the keeper of the land. It's your birthright that makes this land prosper and remain strong."

"Whatever. It doesn't account for you lying to me!"

"I didn't lie to…"

Poppy slaps her hand over his mouth. "YOU did! I asked you about the crops. I said that they seemed better and the hay was sweeter. I've seen the fields glow but thought it was a trick of the sun setting. You said, *country magic*. NOT fae magic. You kept secrets from me. Secrets you should have TOLD me before you bedded me!!"

Rowan pulls her hand off his mouth and wraps both his hands around hers. "I'm sorry. I should have told you, but I stand by my decision that you were not ready."

"But I was clearly ready to be bedded." Poppy pulls her hand back and gestures them away, utter defeat sinking into her body. "Just go. All of you. Get out!"

Rowan stiffens and rises. "If that is your wish."

"It is."

Rowan gives one last look at Poppy, before turning and striding from the house, knowing Daine is following. He stops at the truck and turns. "What do you want, Daine?"

"Nothing. We should leave."

"What about Kaelen?"

"He's probably getting Poppy to send him back as we speak."

"Right. Hop in." Rowan starts the truck and waits until Daine is in. Once he's settled, he backs up and drives back to town in silence.

Kaelen watches the pair leave and moves to kneel in front of Poppy. "Poppy. I know it's a lot to take in, but Rowan has your best interests at heart. Please, just take time and process this. I can't leave like the others. I need to return to the fae realm. Is there anything you want me to pass on to your Grams?"

Poppy looks up, tears flooding from her eyes. "Tell her I am sorry I didn't call more, or come back on my free weekends. That I should never have gone to designer school and that I love her so very much and miss her."

"Come here." Kaelen pulls her out of chair and holds her close, feeling her body shake from the sobs escaping her. "Shh Poppy. I will just tell her you love her. She wanted you to go to school, and she was proud of what you accomplished. Do not feel guilt because you followed your dreams. I guarantee there are no regrets on Rose's side so do not feel regrets on your side. Keep following those dreams. Become the best damn fashion designer the world has seen… But live here. Sign the contract. Commit to Rowan. You both already feel the bond. That much is obvious."

"I will think about it, K-K."

"That's all I can ask for. As an added incentive, remember what I said. Once you sign the contract and bond with Rowan, it guarantees you a place in the faerie realm, where all your ancestors live."

"Wait, so Marie is there? The one who started all this?"

"Correct."

"I am going to have words with her. And with Grams for that damn cock she has outside!"

Kaelen chuckles. "She might have words back. She loved him."

"Yes, well, I might love him as a shish-ka-bob, but knowing my luck, he'd be too tough to chew and still find a way to choke me on the way down."

"I am not telling her that." He admonishes. "How about I just say you don't have the same love for the cock that she did?"

Poppy gasps. "K-K! TMI! And DON'T you dare tell her that! Just let her know we don't get along."

"I will. Are you going to be alright if I leave?"

"Yes. You were supposed to go away with the others."

"It's not me you are mad at, so I figured I would risk it. Don't hold that grudge too long. Rowan is a good person. You will want for nothing if you accept him as your guardian."

"Thanks K-K."

"I could not raise my daughter, but I helped raise you. You are my granddaughter, after all. Now, since all rules have already been broken, I will let you in on a little secret you did *Not* hear from me. The willows out back have their roots in the realm of the fey."

"Wait, the ones with my tire swing?"

"Yes, that's how it's able to hold the weight of the tire and why you, as well as everyone in your lineage are drawn to them. If you touch the tree near the base on the night of a full moon, you might just be able to hear your Grams whisper through the veil."

"Really?"

He places a finger upon her lips. "Shhh, you did not hear that from me."

She smiles, and hugs him tight. "Thank you."

"You're welcome. I love you Poppy."

"I love you too Uncle… Wait, Grandpa K-K."

Kaelen kisses the top of her head and sets her down on the floor, fading away in small motes of light, leaving her alone in the living room. Rising, she heads to the front door and closes it, snapping the lock into place. Padding to the kitchen, she grabs the bottle of wine and pours herself an overfull glass, drinking it as she carries it back to the bedroom. Glaring at the parchment still on her bed, she picks it up and drops it in the box, along with the journal she was reading. Debating on whether to crawl into bed, she glares at Pinecone, still curled up at the foot end. "You can go away too, you treacherous spy."

Pinecone cracks an eye and adjusts her position, but settles back into sleep.

"Right, well, I am not staying in here with you." Turning, she strides from the bedroom and down to the living room, placing her wine on the coffee table. Pulling the throw off the back of the couch, she wraps it around herself and plops herself down on it, staring at the blank TV. She sips her wine as her mind mulls over the day's events, trying to comprehend everything. Resting her head on the armrest, she closes her eyes, tears falling from them at the thought that someone deliberately killed her parents and tried to kill her. That Grams died because of her and no matter what K–K said, she knew it was her fault. She hugs the throw pillow tight, wishing it was her Grams, telling her everything would be alright.

Hours later, she wakes up, disoriented by the sound of a phone ringing. Pushing herself up, she glances at Pinecone curled up at her feet. "Traitor!" Stumbling to her feet, she pads over to the phone and picks it up. "Hello?"

"Hey Poppy. It's Celeste at Everdell Law Offices."

"OH SHIT! I forgot to call. Is it five already? I'm so sorry. It was a really rough day and I must have fallen asleep."

"Hey, it's alright. I figured it must have been something like that or you got busy on the farm. It's not like you are going to run away with one week to go, which is why I called before I left. I didn't want you to lose out on your Gram's inheritance."

"Thanks. I really appreciate that you did that for me." Poppy bursts into tears at the thought of losing the only link she had to Grams. "I'm sorry, I just…"

"Hey, do you want to talk about it? I know I am just someone you call to report in, but I can be a neutral ear to vent to."

"No, it's fine. I just found some of Grams' journals and made the mistake of reading them. I got to my parents' deaths, and it triggered things for me."

"I get it. Well, if you need an ear to listen. I can do that. I will talk to you tomorrow?"

"Yes, I will remember to call."

"Alright. You take care, Poppy. If it makes you feel any better. Us here at the law offices are rooting for you. Especially Mr. Landon's wife."

"His wife?" She asks, confusion lacing her tone. "I don't think I know her."

Celeste chuckles. "You do. Last time she was in here, she said you sold the best damn cockery in town."

"Cockery?..." Poppy laughs. "Oh yes, I remember her. I had to double wrap it for safety's sake because she bought the one of him standing at attention."

"Yes, apparently you impressed her with excellent banter."

"She was fun. I enjoyed that market day."

"Perhaps you will see her again."

"Perhaps. Thanks again for calling me."

"Hey, no worries. If I hadn't, Mr. Landon was going to be stopping by for a house call."

"He would have found me crashed on the couch, oblivious to the outside world."

"Well, I am glad you are alright. Take care Poppy."

"I will. Have a good night." Poppy hangs up the phone, glancing up at the clock and staring at the time that mocked her. 5:15. Sighing, realizing she hasn't taken anything out for dinner, she sorts through the dining pamphlets in the drawer below the phone. She picks one and orders food, heading back to the living room, sipping her warm wine as she waits for dinner. After paying the delivery driver, she picks out a movie and curls up to watch it.

Runway to Ruin

September 22 - 24

The next two days pass in a haze as Poppy drifts aimlessly around the farmhouse, her thoughts whirling at everything Kaelen has explained to her. Her heart breaks within her, wanting both options and yet her mind telling her that the only choice that aligns with everything she has achieved so far, is to sell.

If she sells, she can return to fashion school, and to her dreams of becoming the best damn fashion designer out there, as Kaelen said to do. But he also said to bond with Rowan and stay here. Could she do both? It wasn't feasible in her mind and she had two days to decide whether she should stay and sacrifice her dreams, or sell the farm and break a promise made generations ago.

In the afternoons, she stills as she hears the familiar crunch of Rowan's truck rolling over the gravel, followed by his steady knock at her door. Each thud reminds her of the fields they harvested together, along with the ones still waiting, threatening to spoil if left too long. Feeling his presence as he lingers at the door, waiting for her to answer, before finally giving up and leaving.

Knowing she should open the door or drag her ass to the market, but finding she can't bear the thought of facing him right now. Even if that means feeling the pain strike her heart at the sound of him driving away. A pain that feels as if her world is being ripped apart, which ends up with her in tears on her Gram's bed, clutching her pillows. Seeking comfort from her Grams that only her room can give her right now, with her knick-knacks on the nightstands and dresser, each sitting on perfectly white lace doilies. Even the quilted rooster bedspread wrapped around her is comforting, despite hating the cock outside and not willing to admit that even he has grown on her.

After a few days of being non-existent, Poppy pushes herself up and sits on the edge of the bed, staring at the pieces of a life she's not prepared to pack away. Knowing that if she sells the farm, she'll have to sort through it all, the thought of which makes her stomach twist.

Rising, she moves to the dresser, her fingers trailing over the delicate carvings on the old jewelry box, one that Grams had said was her ancestors' and that she would eventually inherit. A wry smile crosses her lips at the thought that, indeed, she had, with all the jewelry inside. Lifting the lid, she sifts through the pieces, caressing her fingertips over necklaces, rings, and brooches, her thoughts drifting back to when she recalled her Grams wearing them. For years, she assumed they were costume jewelry, but now, knowing what is in her Grams' accounts, she wonders if they are much more valuable and if she should get them appraised.

Placing them back, she turns her attention to the rooster figurine sitting on the opposite corner and picks it up gently. She turns it over and traces the name etched into the bottom. Kaelen. Her uncle K-K and yet, he wasn't. He was her grandfather. Grandpa K-K. Frustration floods her inside as she realizes the signs have always been there.

After the car crash, it was always K-K to her rescue when she scraped a knee, or fell in the fields. He was always there when Grams needed him, no matter the size of the task, from getting something out of the cupboard over her head, to working the fields. Then there is the fact that

K–K is more than he appeared to be, and not just in relations with her and her Grams. The fact that he is a fae, just like Rowan.

She sets the rooster down carefully, and glances around the room, realizing just how blind she had been growing up. Yes, she was young, but clearly she was too absorbed in herself to see what was happening here. Moving to the window, she sits down in the old chair and stares out onto the fields, seeing the stalks of hay they missed blowing in the breeze. Her eyes drift over to the willows by the river, instinctively knowing Rowan is beneath them watching the house, waiting for her decision.

Pulling the curtains closed, she stares at the cream fabric, and for a fleeting moment, her thoughts drift to the outfit she could create with it. Shaking herself from the distraction, she rises, suddenly desperate to get out of the house. Running down the stairs, she grabs the truck keys, then hesitates, something that was too automatic for her these past few weeks. Her fingers tighten around the metal before she drops them back into the dish. Instead, she picks up her car keys and heads into the garage.

Opening the garage door, she backs her car out and gets out to close it after her, since the truck is the one with the garage remote. Returning to her car, she gets in. As she shifts into drive, a flicker of movement in her rearview mirror catches her attention, but she opts to ignore it, suspecting it's Rowan, Daine, or one of their spies.

She presses on the gas, heading down her driveway, but instead of turning right into town, she veers left, away from everything. She drives past the distant houses and rolling farmland, with the occasional scattering of trees growing denser as she approaches the lake. The sign tugs at the memory of her ride on Ebonwind to get there, with Rowan's arms wrapped around her waist, his scent surrounding her and their first kiss upon its shores. Her fingers tighten around the wheel as she pushes the thought away.

Poppy keeps driving, winding through back roads, letting the quiet of the open road soothe her. An hour later, she finds herself at a crossroads and stops to scan the unfamiliar intersection. A large wooden sign looms ahead. *Leaving Everdell.* Frowning, she glances in the rearview mirror, her heart skipping at the sign she hadn't noticed herself passing. *Entering*

Everdell. She shivers, squinting her eyes in the rearview mirror, certain she saw a flicker of black movement in the shadows.

Her thoughts drift to Kaelen's words, recalling his talk of the dark court. Something he never fully explained because there were other matters that needed to be covered. But hadn't her Grams read her something when she was younger, from one of the faerie books she loved? Something about the 'tween spaces, where both light and dark could access it and protections didn't exist?

A cold sweat breaks over her skin as she glances between the signs, knowing instantly that she is sitting in one of those spaces, just like her parents were, right before the logging truck crashed into them. With shaking hands, she presses the gas, and turns the wheel, making a U-turn in the intersection when the car sputters and stalls.

Heart pounding, she twists the key in the ignition and taps on the gas. "Come on baby, start. Don't do this!" The engine turns over, grabs for a second, then sputters and dies again. Slamming her palm against the dash, she fights to control the rising panic as she fumbles to start the car again. Closing her eyes, she takes a few deep breaths, trying to calm herself down. Cars break down all the time… *But not in the 'tween,* her thoughts replied.

Opening her eyes, she glances left up the hill, right down the hill, then into her rearview mirror. A scream rips from her mouth at the monster staring back at her. Spinning in her seat, she sees nothing behind her, just the empty road that leads back to the safety of Everdell. Every fiber in her body telling her to get out of the car and get back on Everdell soil.

Grabbing the handle, she yanks on it to open the door, finding it jammed. "No!" She slams her hand down on it, trying to get it to loosen, registering the glint of metal up the hill in the periphery of her vision. Snapping her eyes up, she stares in horror at the logging truck barreling down the hill towards her.

A strangled cry escapes her lips as she fumbles with the seatbelt, yanking at it until it releases. She scrambles into the backseat and tries those doors, finding them locked too. "Oh gawd, please let me out of this car." She shudders in terror at the trucker's horn blaring, knowing in less than a minute he will run her over, just like her parents. "Please. Don't let me die."

Her gaze darts around the car, frantically trying to figure a way out. Ripping the headrest free from the passenger seat, she grips the padding and slams the metal rods against the window, hope filling her as it cracks. Putting all her weight into it, she drives the metal into the window again. The glass falls around her, drawing a panicked laugh to her lips, just as the horn blares a second time.

Scrambling out of the car, she ignores the sting of fresh cuts on her hands and arms from the glass, stumbling back towards the side of the road. Collapsing to her knees, she covers her head at the sound of twisting metal and shattering glass behind her. "Rowan. Please. Help me. I accept the bonding." Agony lances through her side and back as something sharp embeds itself into her flesh.

"You should not have escaped."

Her breath hitches as a low raspy voice to her left draws her gaze upwards. She shudders in terror as they land on the creature from her rearview mirror, standing beside her with a cruel sneer, its hand lashing out and slapping her across the face.

The sting of its claws ripping her skin open forces her into action. She struggles to her feet and runs towards the sign, needing to get onto Everdell soil, but doesn't make it far before the creature latches onto her and slams her into the ground. She groans as pain floods her, both from the impact and the monster's claws shredding her skin.

Determined not to let him win, she rolls over and kicks him in the face, knocking it away from her while screaming at the top of her lungs. "ROWAN WYNTHORN!" Relief washes over her at the small motes of light forming beside her, knowing he is going to save her.

Rowan materializes in front of her, his stance already defensive, his dangerous gaze locking onto the creature. In one swift motion, he steps forward, planting himself over her, feet on either side of her trembling form, while calling forth a pair of daggers. "She's not yours to take. Step aside unseelie."

"She's mine. She left Everdell unbound."

Rowan narrows his eyes. "Then I would like to see you take her from me."

Another materializes behind the unseelie. "And me."

Realizing they outnumber him, the unseelie tries to fade away, but not before Rowan and Daine rip it to shreds, sending a message back to the dark court with its dead body.

Rowan kneels down beside Poppy, drawing her into his arms while Daine helps the truck driver. "What were you doing out here?"

"I'm sorry. I was driving. I needed to get away from everything and didn't realize where I was. I tried to go back…" She bursts into tears and shakes uncontrollably in his arms. "But then my car just stopped, right there. It wouldn't start. I couldn't get out because the handles were stuck. Like something locked them, but not. I heard the truck's horn, and I heard it run over my car, just like my parents. Just like before. The monster… he was in the mirror…"

"Shhh, you got out, that's what matters. Now, we need to get you to the hospital and get you looked at."

"I broke the window… It was the only way."

"That was smart."

"I'm sorry." Her eyes close, and she slips into darkness as his comfort and scent wraps around her.

Rowan caresses her cheek gently, grateful that she used his full name or they would have been too late. He had panicked when he felt her stepping, or rather, driving over the boundary, the connection between them fading as she did. He turns to Daine, who is helping the truck driver over to the side of the road. "She needs a doctor. She's pretty beat up."

"Ambulance is on the way. I called it in before I got here."

The driver glances over at the pair of them. "She's lucky to be alive. I couldn't stop, my steering and brakes failed me. I blared my horn to get her to move."

"She apparently tried to, but her car died."

"Damn, that's some bad luck on both our parts."

"Or good luck. You both survived."

"Well, when you look at it that way, you might be right. Names Jed."

"Rowan. That there is Daine, and this is Poppy."

"How did you come to be in the area?"

"Out riding horses together. Heard the metal crunching."

"Right. Well, I appreciate it. My airbags must have knocked me out or something."

"Yes. You should make sure you don't have a concussion." Rowan tilts his head, listening to the sound of the ambulance in the distance. "They should be here soon."

Daine gives a nod to them both, sending a knowing look towards Rowan. "You ride with her and I will get the horses back to the farm. Call me later when you need a lift home. I can bring the truck around."

"I will. Thanks Daine."

Daine turns and jogs into the bush, fading into motes of light once he's out of sight.

Hours later, a steady beep... beep... beep... pulls Poppy from the depths of unconsciousness. Her body feels heavy, weighed down by exhaustion and the dull ache radiating through her body. The air is thick with a sterile scent of antiseptic, and the too-bright fluorescent lights push through her closed eyelids. She shifts slightly, wincing as pain lances through her backside, and she hears the soft murmur of voices to her left.

"...She's lucky to be alive," Clara murmurs, her voice filled with concern. "The EMTs told me she was unconscious in your arms when they arrived. What even happened, Rowan? They found you by the Everdell sign. Her car totaled and she was covered in gashes. The police think she must have crawled out through the window before the crash, but...the wounds don't match. They look..."

"Like an animal attack," he finishes for her, his tone unreadable.

"Yes, but the EMTs didn't find any tracks. No sign of a coyote, a bear... nothing. Just you holding Poppy as she bled out on the side of the road and the truck driver." Frustration evident in her voice.

"I know. She was awake when I arrived. Said her car stalled, and the door jammed. That she had to break her way out." Pain floods Rowan's voice, having felt the panic she did being trapped in the car, the same way her parents were, despite not being bonded yet. "I should have talked..." He stops himself from thinking about what might have happened. He had arrived in time, and that's what he needed to focus on.

"Talked about what? If you know something, tell me. Because none of this makes sense. Even Josh the lawyer was asking about her."

"We had a disagreement and she…"

Poppy swallows against the dryness in her throat, trying to push past the fog in her mind, remembering the car caging her in, the truck barreling down upon her and the claws of the creature that wasn't human, trying to kill her. "Rowan?"

Immediately, Rowan is at her side, his hand clutching hers. "I'm here Poppy."

Clara is on her feet in an instant, taking her other hand. "Hey, take it easy, okay? You're in the hospital."

Poppy forces her eyes open, blinking against the harsh lights. Her vision swims, but she finds Rowan first, immediately taking in his haggard appearance, from the dark circles beneath his eyes to the pale skin and fear etched into his features. She cracks a half smile his way. "I think this is the first time I have seen you look like shit."

Rowan squeezes her hand. "I feel like shit. Thank you very much, and you don't look so great yourself."

"Thanks." She rolls her eyes and turns to Clara. "Clara…"

Clara leans over the bed, her worry shifting into full-on exasperation. "You better have a good explanation for this, because I swear, Pops, you have the worst luck of anyone I know."

"I just went for a drive and my car broke down."

"What were you doing out of town?"

"I didn't realize I was that far out…" Poppy manages a weak smile, but her gaze flicks back to Rowan. His grip on her hand grounding, soothing her. He came for her, just like she knew he would. Her eyelids droop and sleep claims her once more.

The next morning, Poppy wakes up feeling disoriented, her eyes landing on the white ceiling above her as memories flood her. Sweeping her gaze around the room, she notices Rowan sitting in a chair, looking worse than he did yesterday. "Rowan?"

His eyes snap open. "Poppy. How are you feeling?"

"What's wrong? You look worse today than yesterday."

Rowan moves over to the bed and clasps her hands. "Not being in Everdell is taking its toll on me."

"But Kaelen said you could manage a few weeks if we went on holidays."

"If bonded, yes. But we have not completed it and…"

Her eyes narrow, realizing there is more to his words than he is saying, suspecting the six weeks Grams gave her was a timeline to get the bonding done. "Wait, how long do we have?"

"By the end of day today."

Poppy struggles to sit up while swinging her legs around to hang off the bed. "Well, we have to go then."

"You can't. They are keeping you in for observation since they surgically removed the metal and glass fragments from your back and stitched up some of the claw wounds."

"I don't care, Rowan. I am not having you fade away because of my mistake." She scans around, spotting the red button nearby and presses it, waiting impatiently as a nurse arrives. She lifts her gaze to the woman walking in, her hair tied in a tight bun and dressed in pale blue scrubs.

"Ms. McInnes, you should still be lying down."

"I need to check out."

"The doctor hasn't approved it."

Poppy snaps at her. "Well, get him to approve it. I need to get back to Everdell."

She shakes her head. "I think you should lie back down. Let me help you."

"No. I don't want to lie down. I want to go home."

"I'm not sure that's advisable. Someone needs to watch over you." The nurse glances over to Rowan, who nods.

"I will care for her. Just give me her meds along with instructions and I will make sure she takes them and gets the rest she needs."

"Fine. I will let Dr. Hummer know."

"Thank you."

Several hours later, after going through all the paperwork and instructions, Poppy dresses in new clothes and staggers out the door with the help of Rowan. He lifts her into the truck and buckles her in. "Hang tight Poppy. It shouldn't take us too long to get back."

She nods and slumps back, her head lolling against the headrest as exhaustion tugs at her. The truck shifts as Rowan climbs into the driver's seat, and she manages a small smile. "Thank you."

"You're welcome," he murmurs, starting the engine. "Now, let's get you home."

"My home or yours?" She teases him, her voice drowsy as the medication settles in.

"Where do you want to go?"

She ponders it for a moment. "Hmm… does yours have a noisy cock that'll wake me up in the morning?"

Rowan chuckles, glancing at her with a smirk. "Nope. But I can't guarantee another kind won't."

Poppy giggles, reaching out to swat his shoulder. "Not allowed. Doctor's orders remember. Only strictly boring rest for at least a week."

"True," he concedes, shifting gears as they pull onto the road. "Guess I'll just have to behave."

"Doubtful," she mumbles, her eyelids fluttering shut, a soft smile still lingering on her lips.

Autumn Ever After

December 15

Months later, Poppy sits out back with her cup of coffee, staring at the rooster preening himself happily on top of the shed. That was one cock that had been mysteriously quiet since she bonded with Rowan and he moved into the farmhouse with her. She knows Rowan had something to do with it with his fae abilities, allowing her to sleep in to a more reasonable hour.

Her thoughts drift back to the ceremony they had beneath the willows, one with Daine officiating it. Feeling the magic in the air wrap around them as they removed Grams' name off the contract and placed Poppy's signature on it. With both of them swearing an oath to each other and exchanging a drop of blood to bind them together forever. At least until the contract gets transferred to the new guardian and keeper, which would be their kids when they are ready to have them. Later though.

First, she needed to hit the runways of the fashion industry hard. Then they could discuss children. She made a promise to K-K and Grams. One she intended to fulfill. Afterwards, Daine had bid her farewell and tears were spilled as he returned to his realm, being no longer needed as a guardian.

Her eyes drift to the chickens as she sips her coffee, wandering around without a care in the world, knowing exactly how they felt because she was feeling it right now. Movement draws her gaze upwards, smiling at the sight of Rowan leading Ebonwind out of the barn for some freedom in the fields after locking him up for last night's storm.

Feeling the link between them, Rowan shifts his gaze to hers and smiles. Leading his horse over to where she sits, he ignores the hens' dismayed clucks at being disturbed. "Finally dragged your lazy ass out of bed, I see."

"Yes, well… City girl here and you spoil me by letting me sleep in."

"Only until spring. Then it's farm work for you, Little Miss Fashionista. How did your Zoom call go with Amber last night?"

"Great. Since I'm bound to farm life now…"

"And me?"

Her voice softens. "Yes, and you… We are teaming up and combining our talents. She can handle the city when I can't, and I'll focus on the sewing and designs when she's too busy. We even brainstormed names last night. First, we thought of McVon, but it sounded too much like McD's. So we flipped it to VonInnes, but it wasn't catchy enough. In the end, we decided on Pombér. It's stylish, unique, and we both love it, so that's the name we are going with."

Rowan chuckles. "That it is…"

Poppy narrows her eyes at him. "I sense a but."

Leaning in, he brushes a kiss against her lips and murmurs, "I just figured with two hens running the show, you'd have worked a cock into the name somewhere."

Poppy laughs. "Trust me, we thought about it!"

"I bet you did."

"In all languages even. I didn't know that Jean-Pierre Coq is actually Jean-Pierre rooster. Amber and I laughed hard at that one."

"Pretty sure I heard it in my dreams last night. The hens cackle summoning some sort of spirits. Now, did you want to go for a ride and see what damage the storm did last night, or are you heading off to disappear in your sewing studio?"

"Sure. I will take a ride." She places her coffee cup on the deck and rises, slipping her arms around his waist and snuggling in. "Then afterwards, perhaps we can have an indoor ride."

Rowans nods, wrapping his arms around her, feeling desire flood him at the woman pressed up against him. His bonded keeper and his love. Kissing the top of her head, his lips curve into a smile. "Perhaps I could be persuaded."

She laughs. "Like it's hard!"

"Oh, it already is. Trust me."

"Rowan!" A deep blush crosses her cheeks as her eyes drop to verify his words.

He tightens his hold. "What. I can't help it. I love you."

"I love you too, Rowan."

The End

Cock-a-doodle-doo

J ust because.

When a rooster tells a story, it's hard to beat.

He's got the loudest crow in the barnyard.

That's one cock that won't back down from a fight.

He's got stamina, goes all night and is still up at sunrise.

Careful, my cock's got a temper—mess with him and he'll go off.

A little attention, and my cock perks right up.

It's not the size of the cock in the fight, but the size of the fight in the cock.

Why did the rooster cross the road?

To prove to the hens he had the biggest cock-a-doodle-doo in town!

Why did the rooster strut across the barnyard?

Because he heard the hens love a cocky attitude!

Why did the rooster refuse to fight?

He didn't want to ruffle his own feathers. His ego was already big enough!

People of Everdell

Poppy-Cock Farm
Poppy McInnes - MC
Rose Levens - Grams
Callum Levens - Gramps
Aisley McInnes - Mom
Malcolm McInnes - Dad
Reginald - Rooster
Pinecone - Cat

Everdell Law Offices
Josh Landon - Lawyer
Celeste - Secretary

Townsfolk
Mrs Plum - Teacher
Clara Dunmere - High School Bestie

Melody Strutter – High School Nemesis
Bernie – Gas Station Attendant
Barney Jackson – Neighbour
Astrid Winters – Hay Buyer
Barb – Cloth Depot
Sharon – Everdell Reality

Outside Everdell
Dr Hummer – Hospital
Amber Vontaine – College Bestie

Fae Guardians
Rowan Wynthorn
Ebonwind – His bonded Friesian Horse
Kaelen Stormvale
Daine Cairos
– Also known as Danial – Farm hand
– Also known as Cyrus – Janitor
Rook – His bonded Crow
Marie Melantine – Ancestor

August

SUN	MON	TUE	WED	THU	FRI	SAT
						1
2	3	4	5	6	7	8
9	10	11	12	13	14	15 Poppy Arrives
16 Funeral	17	18	19	20	21 World Fashion Show	22
23	24 Market	25	26	27	28	29
30	31					

September

Sunday	Monday	Tuesday	Wednesday	Thursday	Friday	Saturday
		1	2	3	4	5 Hen Party
6 Hen Party	7 Hen Party	8	9	10	11	12
13	14	15	16	17	18	19 Harvest Moon Festival
20	21	22	23	24	25	26 6 Wks
27	28	29	30			

Contributors

Thank you to everyone involved !

Cover Design - Marta at Getcovers
Inside Roosters – Royalty-Free Dover Clip art
Beta readers - M Veronneau, E Carter, E McMonnies, C Lewis
Editor - E McMonnies, C Lewis
Editing Software - Free version of ProWritingAid, Google Docs with Grammarly, Atticus.
Assists - M Harris, B Whittome, H Roberts
Author Portrait – G Woodward
For Fun – Chapter heading font is Henny Penny

Additional Information

Thank you for taking the time to read my stories and I hope that you enjoyed them. If you enjoyed them, below is a list of my other books. Please feel free to follow me, or add me via Goodreads or Facebook. Also, reviews are important to self published authors, so please take the time to leave one. Thank you.

Social media – www.facebook.com/AuthorRandiAnneDey
www.facebook.com/groups/randiswriting
www.goodreads.com/author/show/45347028.Randi_Anne_Dey
The King's Mystic: Oct 2023
The Dragon's Mystic: May 2024
Cantara's Mystic: Apr 2025
Madison's Web: Mar 2024
Dragonscales Divide: Nov 2024
Chahaya Durmada: Five Swords of Power: Eta 2025
Fae Guardians Poppy: May 2025
You Stole my Shroom: Fall 2025
Royal Deception: Tails Scales and Tiaras Anthology June 2024
The Emperor's Violet: Cabs and Crime Eta 2025

About the Author

Randi lives in Victoria, BC. Canada. She is a dog groomer by day and a writer/gamer/reader by night. She partook in the SCA and taught medieval dance for nearly fifteen years. Since 2004, she has attended a Faerie festival yearly, keeping fantasy alive in her heart. With four books published, she hopes they will draw you away from the modern world and into a land of intrigue and fantasy, where magic, dragons, shifters, vampires and kings roam the lands.

9 781069 248466